Puffin Books
Super Gran

Super Gran Smith hurled herself at Young Willard's football in a sliding tackle. 'Come on, laddie, give us a wee kick at your ball!' she cried. Willard stared at her, amazed, for only a minute ago she had been just an ordinary, little, old white-haired lady sitting on a park bench. But that was before the strange beam of blue light shot through her, which was the start of Super Gran, a being with incredible strength, fantastic speed and X-ray eyes.

But it was Edison who knew that Gran's miracle powers had come from a machine invented by her father, and now stolen by the unscrupulous Inventor, and she wanted the new Super Gran to help her get it back.

So begin the riotous adventures of Super Gran, Willard and Edison, and their attempts to foil the Inventor's plan to create an army of Supermen who will help him take over and rule the world. Daunted by nothing, whether a bank raid, a drowning child or an attempted kidnapping, Super Gran with her amazing skills and high spirits hurtles from one event to the next. Gathering a force of Super-Oldies, she goes forward to battle with the Inventor and his Super-Toughies.

Readers of about nine and over will enjoy this very funny story.

SUPER GRAN

Forrest Wilson
illustrated by David McKee

PUFFIN BOOKS

To Granny Min – who inspired Super Gran

Puffin Books, Penguin Books Ltd, Harmondsworth,
Middlesex, England
Penguin Books, 625 Madison Avenue,
New York, New York 10022, U.S.A.
Penguin Books Australia Ltd, Ringwood,
Victoria, Australia
Penguin Books Canada Ltd, 2801 John Street,
Markham, Ontario, Canada L3R 1B4
Penguin Books (N.Z.) Ltd, 182–190 Wairau Road,
Auckland 10, New Zealand

First published by Andersen Press Ltd 1978
Published in Puffin Books 1980
Reprinted 1980 (twice)

Made and printed in Great Britain by
Richard Clay (The Chaucer Press) Ltd,
Bungay, Suffolk

Contents

1 Gran and Super Gran

Granny Smith, an ordinary, little, old white-haired lady, resting on a seat in the public park, began to feel decidedly peculiar....

Granny Smith was old and her eyesight and hearing were not as good as they used to be; she needed glasses with extra-thick lenses, and she needed a hearing-aid.

Her poor, thin old body was stiff and full of rheumatism, and her legs were weak; she needed a walking-stick to help her get along. She felt the cold so much, even in summer, that she had to wrap up well; so she was wearing a thick coat, a scarf and a tartan tammy.

Her arms were so frail that she couldn't carry even the lightest shopping-bag, so she used a shopping-trolley. And she *so* hated being seen with it – she said it made her look old!

So here she sat, resting on a park bench because she could walk only a few hundred yards at a time, without getting completely tired out. Her grandson, freckle-faced Willard, whom she called Willie, for short, had accompanied her to the park, but he'd left her to rest while he played football with some of his pals, a few yards away. Willard wore, as he always did, a football shirt in the red-and-white stripes of his local League team.

Suddenly...a beam of blue light shot out of nowhere,

it seemed, and struck the little old lady. It engulfed her and the seat, for about a minute, and then it faded and disappeared, as suddenly as it had appeared.

And it was then that Granny Smith began to feel peculiar. And it was that one minute which changed her life completely. For that was the start of SUPER GRAN....

It was also just about then that the girl, Edison Faraday Black, appeared on the scene. She came rushing down a grassy slope towards Granny Smith, shouted something excitedly...and then tripped, as she always seemed to do, fell and rolled headlong down the slope, ending up at Granny Smith's feet.

The auburn-haired girl stood up and dusted herself down. 'Are you all right, lady?' she asked, concerned. 'I saw the ray hit you and....'

Granny Smith, feeling *most* peculiar by now, put her hand to her head. 'Aye...I...I think so, lassie....'

The little old lady wasn't really sure. What *was* happening, she wondered. For something definitely *was* happening to her. Something strange. She could feel it in her bones; she could feel it all through her thin, frail body.

'It was that rotter, the Inventor, I *know* it was, it must have been,' Edison said, as she looked all around, towards the dozen or so large houses nearby which backed on to the public park. 'I know he lives round about here *some*where.' She frowned. 'And I've *al*most caught up with him. I just wish I knew which house was his.' She looked determined. 'But I'll *find* him, don't worry!'

Granny Smith couldn't take all this nonsense in. Not right then. She felt faint. Then, suddenly, she felt the opposite – 'un-faint' – whatever *that* meant, she thought.

She felt terrible, and then, suddenly, she felt great! It was all very mysterious, and confusing. So she was too concerned with all these mixed feelings to be bothered listening to the girl's ramblings – or her 'bletherings' as she, Granny Smith, would have called them.

Her eyes, her ears, her bones, joints, limbs all seemed to be 'popping'. It was decidedly queer. It wasn't so much 'pains' she was having, it was 'sniap', she thought.

'"Sniap"? What's "sniap"?' she wondered, out loud.

'Pardon?' Edison frowned.

Granny Smith giggled. '"Sniap" is "pains" backwards! The *opposite* of "pains",' she explained to the girl. 'I'm having lots of lovely "sniap"!' She had just invented the word and was extremely proud of her cleverness. She could never have thought of anything like that before this happened.

She had a kind of mist in front of her eyes, so she pulled her glasses off – and found she could see perfectly! She threw them away and they landed on the nose of a little white poodle, sniffing around some bushes...FIFTY YARDS AWAY!

She listened. She could hear the boys' shouts deafeningly loud; she could hear the sparrows in the distant tree-tops, chirping as if they were sitting on her shoulder! So she pulled her hearing-aid off and tossed

9

it away, too. And it hit the little, be-spectacled poodle on the head!

Granny Smith stood up, smiled – and bent down to touch her toes; something she hadn't been able to do for about thirty years!

'Are…are you *sure* you're all right?' Edison asked, frowning. 'Oh! Careful! What're you doing?' She moved towards Granny Smith to steady, or catch her, if she fell.

But the little old lady didn't need her help. 'I'm…I'm not sure, lassie,' she said, as she straightened up. Then she grinned, hugely. 'Aye…aye…I *am* sure. I *am* all right. I'm *more* than all right. I'm terrific! Yippee!'

She yelled with delight, did a little jig, kicked her heels together, threw her tartan tammy into the air, jumped about…and threw her walking-stick away! 'I won't be needing *that* thing again!'

The little white poodle, glasses on its nose and the hearing-aid strung over its back, saw the stick flying towards it…and ran for its life!

Things were happening too quickly for Edison, however. Only a few minutes ago she'd been hovering at the top of the grassy slope, near the park railings, when she'd seen Granny Smith walking slowly and painfully along, leaning on her walking-stick and clutching at the arm of her grandson, who had been trailing the shopping-trolley along. And now, after only one little shot from the machine's ray, Edison was looking at a miracle! 'So it *does* work on people!' she murmured to herself.

She felt a surge of pride in her father, at the thought

10

of his machine working; it definitely *was* a Super-machine! But then she had another surge – of anger, for the hated Inventor, who had stolen it from him.

Edison came out of her daydream when she realized that Granny Smith was looking towards the boys, and was saying: 'I'm away to have a game of football, lassie! Are you coming?' Her eyes gleamed.

'Oh no!' the girl gasped. 'Maybe you're not…uh…I mean, maybe you're not strong enough yet for that, and besides….'

'Blethers!' The old lady took off her heavy winter coat and threw it over the bench; and the scarf followed. Then she put her tartan tammy on at a jaunty angle, as she ran to join the boys. 'Of *course* I'm strong enough for a silly wee game of football. Who says I'm not! What d'you think I am…a little old lady?'

'But you *are* a little old la…!' The girl shrugged. What was the use?

Edison picked up the coat and scarf, took the handle of the trolley, and started to trot after the old lady. She knew she would never catch up with her, for Granny Smith was now giving a good imitation of an Olympic sprinter, as she sped towards the boys.

As she trotted, Edison tried to explain: 'It was my dad, you see…at least, to begin with…then the budgie escaped…and that rotten Inventor pinched it…the machine, I mean, not the budgie!…and it was *he* who must've hit you with the Super-ray just now…and it was the ray which made you….'

But the girl was muttering to herself, for Granny Smith was now hundreds of yards away, catching up with the boys' game of football.

The old lady reached the boys and she threw herself forward in a sliding tackle, the way she'd seen the footballers on the telly doing. Her foot touched the ball and nudged it away from the boy who had it.

'Come on, laddie, give us a wee kick at your ball!' she said.

'Eh?' the boy gasped.

Willard, nearby, was also taken aback. 'Hey! Gran?' But only for a second. Then he recovered his wits and went flying after her, in hot pursuit.

Willard was football-mad. He would play football any*where*, with any*thing* for a ball, and with any*one*! He'd play with boys, men, girls…grannies, even!

'Hey! Gran! Come back!' he yelled, as he chased her. As if she would! A miracle had happened and Willard's little old granny was chasing a football; and nothing, and no one, would stop her!

'Come on, Willie, laddie – catch me!' she challenged him.

The faster Willard ran after his gran, the faster she ran away from him, dribbling about, the ball at her feet as if it were tied to her old-fashioned shoe-laces.

Willard at last caught up with her and was just about to get his foot to the ball, when the old lady neatly side-stepped and dribbled it away from him again. The boy went slithering on, stopped, came back…and his gran beat him again! He just couldn't get *near* the ball, let alone get it away from her.

After five or six attempts, Willard began to get a bit annoyed. For Willard was a very good footballer. He

12

played for his school team and his boys' club team…and he wasn't used to being out-dribbled, out-played and out-manoeuvred in a game. Especially by an old lady! Especially in front of his pals. That was the embarrassing part of it. That's what really annoyed him.

So, forgetting for the moment *who* she was, he gave his opponent an extra-fierce shoulder-charge, knocking her off-balance.

'Hey! Foul, ref!' Granny Smith cried, and then, regaining her balance, she decided that two could play rough!

She nudged him – gently, she thought! – with her bony shoulder…and sent him flying through the air! 'Take that, Willie, you scunner!' she grinned. And poor Willard crashed to the ground, winded – ten yards away!

'Oof!' he groaned.

'Oh, I'm sorry, Willie,' Gran apologized, eyes twinkling, as she ran to help him to his feet. 'Are you all right, son?'

'Y–yes th–thanks,' Willard stammered, not hurt – but surprised!

He had never seen anything like this before, and neither had his pals, who could only stand and stare, open-mouthed, unable to believe their eyes! A granny – a frail old, weak old granny who could play football like that. She was super!

His chest puffed out with pride, Willard grinned over at his pals. He was proud of her. 'I'm goin' to get you into my teams, Gran,' he said, forgetting he'd have a job getting a little old lady into boys' football teams!

Just then, Edison came running up to the group. Running wasn't something she was good at – tripping was more in her line! – and Willard, his gran and the boys had easily left her behind. Besides, hadn't she to struggle along with the old lady's trolley and coat?

'Are you all right?' Edison asked, sure the old lady couldn't possibly be.

'Sure. Fine, thanks!' Willard replied. 'Just a bit winded.' He grinned. 'Hey! I'm goin' to get Gran into my football teams, and....'

'Not *you,* stupid!' Edison retorted, glaring at him. 'I meant the old lady.' She turned to her. 'Are *you* all right?'

Granny Smith looked puzzled. 'Who – me?' She stood there, quietly tapping the ball back and forward from one foot to the other. 'Jings, lassie, why shouldn't I be? What's wrong with me?'

'Well...I mean...all that running about, playing football and...and everything. I mean, well...you *are* an old lady, you know....' Edison was worried in case the old lady strained herself.

'An old lady!' Granny Smith was indignant. 'Blethers! I'm as fit as *you* are.' She looked Edison up and down, and thought better of what she had said. 'In fact, lassie, I'm a lot fitter! But don't ask me to explain how it happened!'

'But *I* can tell you...' Edison began.

But Granny Smith wasn't listening. She gave the ball a hefty kick. 'Come on, laddies, who's for another wee game, eh?'

The ball went flying hundreds of yards through the

14

air…towards a certain terrified, little white poodle!

'And this time,' Granny Smith grinned at Edison, 'I want *every*one to join in!'

'Oh no!' Edison groaned.

'Oh, and by the way,' Granny Smith commanded, 'from now on I want you all to call me SUPER GRAN. 'Cos that's what I am, amn't I? A Super Gran!'

And that was just the *start* of the adventures of SUPER GRAN.

2 The Inventor, Tub and the Machine

Edison was right – it *was* the Inventor who had been responsible for little old Granny Smith becoming Super Gran. And the reason it happened was because Einstein, the cat, had got in the way.

The Inventor was a middle-aged man with a shock of thick, black hair and thick, black eyebrows...and he wasn't much of an inventor! His big ambition in life was to rule the world, no less! He had devised some inventions to give him the power to do this and when they had failed he had taken to stealing Edison's dad's inventions instead. His idea was to use the Super-machine to turn ordinary men into Supermen who would form into an army, to help him take over the world.

But something had gone wrong.

The Inventor's assistant was an untidy, not-too-bright, fat teenager called Tub, who was perpetually hungry. And Tub now had a most important role to play for the Inventor. For the time had come to try out the machine and the Inventor was going to try it out on Tub!

He stood the youth against a wall, inside his workshop, which was a back room of his house; he pointed the gun-like projector of the machine at him, and he switched it on.

16

'It'll take a few minutes to warm up,' he told Tub. 'And stop shaking so much – I might miss you!'

'I–I–I can't h–help it,' stuttered Tub, nervously, between clenched teeth. 'I'm s–s–scared!'

'Nonsense! There's nothing to be scared of,' the Inventor assured him, heartily – although he didn't know if there was or not!

Tub had definitely *not* volunteered to be the guinea-pig in this experiment. What happened was: the Inventor said: 'Would you like to get the six-months' back-pay I owe you, Tub?' Tub had naturally said: 'Not half!' – he hadn't had any pay at all since he started working with the Inventor – and he found himself facing the Super-machine shaking and quaking with fright!

The Inventor carefully aimed the machine's barrel at Tub and made ready to press the button and pull the switch which would turn Tub into a Super-Tub, capable of doing anything – he hoped!

'Don't worry, Tub,' he assured him again, 'it shouldn't take a minute – and it won't hurt you!'

'H–h–how do *you* know?' Tub asked him. 'You haven't tried it yourself!'

'Oh, don't be such a baby,' his boss scolded. 'Besides, once you're a Super-man you'll be strong and tough, with Super-powers. You'll be able to help me to rule the world. You won't have to keep trying to learn all that karate, judo, kung-fu nonsense!'

Tub spent his spare time reading all the books he could find on self-defence, and it was the thought of all the super-karate and super-kung-fu he'd be able to do that encourged him to go along with the Inventor's plans to make him Super. Plus the six-months' back-pay, of course!

'But I d–d–don't want to help you to rule anything,' Tub protested. Why was his boss always on about ruling the world, he wondered, not for the first time. 'I just w–want me back-pay, that's all.'

'Huh!' the Inventor snorted. 'What will a measly six-months' back-pay be when you're Super and can do Super things?'

Tub had dreamed for years of being a tough guy, like all his television heroes – the wrestlers, the kung-fu experts, the karate-chopping spies. This *would* make being Super an attraction if he could be like them.

The trouble was, Tub *had* tried boxing, wrestling, judo and all the rest of them, was never without a self-defence book in his pocket, but he was no use at any of them. In fact, when he'd tried out his judo on his little sister, *she* had given *him* a black eye! He just couldn't win…not even against a seven-year-old! So, when the Inventor suggested making him Super, this was what persuaded Tub to have a go at it.

'What would you do with all that money anyway?' the Inventor went on. 'You'd just spend it on food and sweets and chocolate and get fatter and fatter.'

Tub looked down at his more-than-ample figure and scowled. 'I'm not fat…it's muscles!'

'Muscles? You're joking!' the Inventor retorted. 'I've seen bigger muscles on mussels!' he laughed, but Tub didn't see the joke.

The shrill ringing of the front doorbell interrupted

the Inventor's laughter. 'Tch! Who's that?'

The ringing continued shrilly, as if a prompt answer was urgently required.

'Mrs Bottomly'll answer it,' the Inventor muttered, too busy with the machine, and referring to his housekeeper.

'B–b–but Mrs Bottomly's out shopping,' Tub said, having second thoughts about the Super-Tub lark. He'd decided he'd rather wait a while before being made Super. Like – ten years, for instance!

He stepped away from the wall. 'Don't worry, boss, I'll go.'

'Oh no you won't. You stay where you are. *I'll* get it.' The Inventor grumbled as he left the room to answer the bell, which was still ringing, continuously. 'It'll be the postman with some gear I was ordering.'

Tub sighed. There was no way out for him. He would just have to stay where he was and go through with it, after all.

He glanced round the big room which the Inventor used as a workshop. There were benches everywhere, full of tools, machines, vices, motors, electric wires and gadgets scattered all over them. As well as the window which Tub stood beside, there was another one, on his right, through which the light shone to operate the machine.

The Inventor had explained the workings of Edison's father's machine to Tub, and how it was operated by the sun and the stars, or 'solar' and 'stellar' energy, as the Inventor had referred to it. But Tub hadn't really understood much of the Inventor's explanation.

Tub, too busy with his thoughts just then, didn't notice that Einstein, the cat, had crept into the room. He padded softly forward and jumped up on to one of the benches, bumping the Super-machine ever-so-slightly as he did so.

'Hi, Einstein,' Tub greeted him. 'Better watch out. Don't come near *me* – or you'll end up as a Super-cat!'

But Einstein had no desire to go near Tub. He was quite content to sit on the bench and wonder what the two crazy humans were up to now.

He had seen a previous invention which the Inventor had tried out; a ray-gun which had back-fired, shooting the ray upwards, by mistake, through the ceiling, the bedroom floor and the Inventor's bed – leaving gaping holes in all three!

And then there was the anti-gravity belt which the Inventor had strapped on to himself, to try out. Something had gone wrong and the Inventor had shot up and down from the floor to the ceiling, without his being able to stop it. Tub had found him, a couple of hours later, held fast against the ceiling, and had had to throw him a strong rope, to pull him down to the floor!

And it was for these reasons that the Inventor now got Tub to try out any new inventions. *He* wasn't going to risk life and limb. The Inventor wasn't daft, altogether!

'It *was* the postman,' said the Inventor, returning with a large parcel. He put it down on the only chair in the room. 'Right then, let's get started.' He went over to operate the machine.

Before Tub could think of any other excuses to delay

the test, the Inventor pressed a button, pulled a switch – and the machine started working.

Lights flashed, sparks sparked, wheels whirred and clanked, and suddenly a blue ray shot out of the machine's gun-barrel...and missed Tub by inches! It shot through the window, across the Inventor's wilderness of a back garden, over the wall at the foot and into the public park at the other side, where, of course, it hit Granny Smith, as she rested on a bench.

But the Inventor didn't realize this had happened. All he knew was that he had operated the machine, the machine had worked – but Tub was still Tub. He wasn't Super-Tub, capable of doing anything – like, for instance, helping him rule the world. No, he was still ordinary, useless Tub, capable of doing practically nothing!

'What went wrong?' he muttered, as Tub sighed with relief, realizing that he was still normal, after all. For Tub was now definitely *not* interested in becoming a Superman. Let him try it out on someone else first, he thought.

'Can I have me back-pay now?' he asked.

'Certainly not!' the Inventor snapped. 'You haven't earned it yet. I'll have to find out what went wrong. I'll have to test the machine, then try it out again. And *then* you'll get your back-pay.'

He added, under his breath, 'When I invent – or pinch – a money-making machine!'

'Huh!' murmured Tub, who hadn't caught this last part.

'I don't understand it,' the Inventor went on, 'it

seemed to work all right. It just didn't seem to affect *you.'* He scratched his head, puzzled. 'And it worked all right with the budgie, too!'

'Eh? Budgie? What budgie?'

'Black's budgie,' the Inventor replied, referring to an experiment of Edison's dad which he had witnessed.

The budgie had accidentally been hit by the Super-machine's ray and had been made Super. It had then yanked the bars of its cage apart with its beak and claws and flown away, at Super-speed, zooming past the Inventor as he stood behind a bush outside Mr Black's workshop window, spying.

The last that was seen of the bird was when it had swooped down to the lawn, picked up a neighbour's cat in its claws and had dropped it, terrified and spitting furiously, on the top-most branch of the tallest tree in the garden! Then it screeched: 'I'm a Super-budgie!' and it zoomed off at Super-speed!

'Eh?' Tub repeated. 'A black budgie?'

'No! Black's budgie,' the Inventor retorted, then remembered he shouldn't tell Tub that he'd been spying on Edison's father and had stolen the machine from him, as he had previously stolen Mr Black's other inventions.

'Who's Black?' Tub asked.

'Oh...ah...no one, never mind.' He changed the subject. 'Let's think about why the machine went wrong.' He paced up and down the workshop, a worried look on his face. 'I can't understand it, Tub. Can't understand it. I pressed the button, and the switch, and....'

He looked over to where Tub was now sweeping the floor, with a brush and shovel, round the foot of the Super-machine. 'Careful, Tub! Mind where you're putting that brush! Don't touch the machine! Careful – you'll move it, and it'll....'

A sudden thought struck him. 'That's it!' he yelled, swinging round. He looked towards the bench where Einstein was curled up, dozing. He thumped his fist into his other palm. 'Einstein – the cat!' he exclaimed.

Tub looked up, stupidly. 'I *know* Einstein's the cat!'

The Inventor ignored him. 'Einstein wasn't there when I left the room, but he's there now!' He paused. 'So *he* must've done it!'

'Oh yes,' Tub agreed. 'Einstein came into the room when you went to answer the door. He jumped up on the bench.'

'Why didn't you tell me?' the Inventor roared. '*He* must have done it.'

'Tell you what?' Tub's mouth hung open. 'Done what?'

'Einstein must've bumped the machine, and moved it. That's what happened. The Super-ray missed you and shot out through the window.' He crossed to the machine and saw that it was, in fact, now pointing towards the window.

He moved the projector back to its original position. 'Come on, Tub, let's try again.'

It was then that Tub had his Great Idea; his unexpected Thought; his Inspiration! And, as Tub never – ever – had *any* ideas, this was quite an occasion!

'Bo–oss...' he began, slowly. But the Inventor

wasn't listening. 'Bo–oss...' he tried again, getting more excited by his Great Idea. He looked out of the window, past the weedy wilderness, the uncut hedges, the 'jungle' lawn and beyond it, over the wall towards the public park. 'Bo–oss...' he began once more, 'I was thinking. Where did the Super-ray go to – if it didn't hit me? Huh?'

'Tub, I told you, be quiet, I'm trying to think....' He stopped and looked at Tub. Then he gaped, in astonishment. For once in his life Tub had actually said something sensible and important!

'I mean,' Tub continued, 'if *I'm* not a Super-man, then someone else might be!'

'Yes...well...ahem...um...' the Inventor stammered, pink with embarrassment. Why had *he* not realized that the ray must have shot out of the window? He was annoyed because Tub *had* thought about it.

So where *had* the ray gone? And *had* it hit someone else?

The Inventor dived to the window, pushing Tub aside.

'It must've gone over there,' Tub said, pointing to the park.

'Yes, yes. I know that, I know that,' the Inventor snapped. 'But there's no harm done. There's no one in sight.' He turned back to the machine, and stopped. 'But someone *could* have been hit by it – and moved away by now....' He dived towards the door. 'Come on – we'll have to find out!'

They rushed out of the house and round to the park

gates, nearby. There was no one in the park who was near the wall at the bottom of the Inventor's back garden; only, far in the distance, a boy, a girl and an old woman, sitting on a park seat.

Tub pointed towards them. 'Why don't we ask *them* about it?'

'Ask them what?' the Inventor scoffed, putting on a mimicking face, and voice: 'Please – did you by any chance see a strange, blue Super-ray floating about out here? 'Cos we've lost one!' He snorted. 'Don't be daft!'

'Well, I only thought,' Tub suggested, 'maybe one of them's a Superman now?'

'Does it look like it? I ask you? An old woman and a couple of kids? Would they be sitting around a park if they were Super? Of course not! They'd be out there ruling the world!' He strode off, back towards the house. 'Come on, we've got work to do. It'll take all afternoon to re-charge the machine's batteries.'

Tub shrugged, and followed him.

What the Inventor didn't realize was that Super Gran had just had a second game of football with the boys, who had now gone to play on the swings; she had had a race with Willard – halfway round the park – and was now having a little bit of a rest...before she decided what Super things she'd do next!

3 A Super Rescue

'What'll we do now?' Super Gran asked. 'We've played football and we've raced and....'

'How about climbing those trees?' Willard suggested, pointing.

'Good idea, laddie.'

'Oh, Super Gran, do you think you should?' Edison asked, concerned in case the old woman might overdo things and end up worse than she had been to start with. 'I think you'd better have a little rest first.'

'I've just *had* a wee rest, lassie!' Super Gran protested.

'I really meant you to have a *long* rest,' Edison admitted.

'Blethers! I've been having long rests for the last thirty years or more! It's time I started *doing* something. Time I started to enjoy myself a wee bit. Isn't that right, Willie?'

Willard winced at being called 'Willie' but nodded agreement with his gran nevertheless. 'Sure is, Gran.' He was eager to get on and play some more with his new-found playmate and was fed-up with all the chat that was going on. Willard hated chat, wanted action.

'Come on, the lads've gone to the swings. Race you there!'

'But maybe your Super-energy'll disappear again,'

Edison warned Super Gran. 'Maybe the ray's effects'll die out. Or reverse. Or something. You might become a little old lady again.' She frowned.

'Don't you worry yourself, dearie,' Super Gran assured the girl. 'I feel that this new strength – this Super-strength – I've got is going to last. I just *know* it is!' She turned to her grandson: 'Right then, Willie, I'll give you another race....'

'To the swings?' he asked, ready to race her.

'No, how about the boating-loch? I feel like going boating!'

'Where?' He was puzzled. 'Oh, the boating-*lake*, you mean?'

'Loch – lake it's all the same,' she grinned. 'I keep forgetting you call things by the wrong names down here in England!' She laughed. She'd lived in England for about forty years now, but she still liked to remind herself – and everyone else – that she was Scottish, at heart. 'Right then – last one there's a silly old scunner!'

Super Gran and Willard went racing away together in the direction of the boating-lake and Edison, as usual, was left behind to carry Super Gran's heavy coat, and trail the shopping-trolley.

'What's a "scunner"?' she asked a nearby sparrow, pecking crumbs off the ground. She shrugged and started to follow them, slowly. 'Must be something Scottish, I suppose.'

'Let's go out in a rowing-boat, Gran,' Willard suggested, when they'd reached the lake.

'Good idea,' she replied, ignoring the strange looks she got from the people she zoomed past – people who had never in their lives seen a little old lady running as fast as *this* little old lady ran. 'Bags me row!' she claimed.

They had to wait in a queue for a while before they got a boat, and when Edison eventually arrived they had just reached the head of it and were jumping into a boat, tied up at the landing-stage.

The boatman, a sour-faced man with grey hair and a drooping, sorrowful moustache, frowned. 'Here, sonny, you're sitting in the wrong seat. You're supposed to sit over there if you're going to row. Move over. Change places with the old lady.'

'But I'm not rowin',' Willard grinned. 'Gran is. That is – my Super Gran is! She bagged first row, see?'

'Huh?' the man grunted. 'Now, look here, sonny, don't be funny with me. How the 'eck can an old lady like that do the rowing?'

'Just watch – and see!' Super Gran grinned.

'Oh, Super Gran, do you think you should?' Edison asked, as she hesitated on the landing-stage, one foot in the boat.

Super Gran took the oars in both hands. 'Aye lassie, of course I should. Why ever not? And do stop blethering, will you, and get in. *If* you're coming with us, that is?'

Edison had realized, while chasing after them, that she had somehow become involved with these people, was tagging along with them, without really having been invited. She wondered if she *should* tag along or not. But then she decided that Super Gran might be able to help her trace the Inventor, and retrieve her dad's

machine. Besides she, in turn, would be able to keep an eye on Super Gran, to make sure that she didn't overdo things. Her grandson certainly wouldn't, that was for sure! So she'd tag along, after all.

She stepped into the boat and took a seat beside Willard, as Super Gran dipped the oars in the water and began to pull back on them.

The boatman had only just released the rope when Super Gran went into her first stroke. She pulled back – and Edison, who had hardly had a chance to take her seat properly, very nearly shot, backwards, out of the boat!

'Blimey!' the boatman exclaimed as the boat zoomed away. He couldn't believe it. 'She must be a blinkin' Olympic oarsman...oarswoman, I mean...or some-thin'!'

Super Gran pulled on the oars another six or seven strokes, and the boat was already almost halfway across the lake – going at speed! And Edison, still not properly seated, had a job to keep herself inside the boat, as it sped along. But Willard was enjoying himself.

'Wow! This is super!' he cried. 'I've never gone so fast in a rowin'-boat before. I'll bet no one has! It's nearly as fast as a motor-boat!'

Edison, holding to the side of the boat, timidly, asked: 'H–how did you learn to row so well, S–super Gr–gran?'

'I don't know, lassie,' Super Gran smiled, 'I've never rowed a boat in my life before! Nor played football either, for that matter! But I've got this feeling I can do anything now. *Any*thing! I don't know how, but I can.

And it's great! It's super!'

'Yes, Super Gran, it was the Super-machine, you see. Let me tell you about it...' she began, but Willard interrupted, pointing.

'Look!' he yelled. 'Someone's fallen out of that boat over there!'

'Where?' Super Gran looked round, saw a small blonde head bobbing up and down in the water, dropped her oars – and stood up!

'Super Gran!' Edison gasped. 'What are you doing?'

'I'm going to save that wee lassie, that's what I'm doing,' she replied, holding her arms out, ready to dive into the water.

'But you can't, Super Gran!' Edison cried. 'Can you swim?'

'Super Gran shrugged. 'Never tried! But here goes...!'

'Row the boat over, Gran,' Willard suggested.

'Too slow!' Super Gran dived head-first into the water.

'Super Gran – come back – you'll be drowned!' Edison turned to Willard. 'Now *we'll* have to rescue *her*!'

'Rescue Gran? Super Gran? You're jokin'! Just look at her!'

Edison looked, and saw to her amazement that Super Gran was cutting through the water, with perfect strokes, like an Olympic champion. And she was already halfway to the little girl.

'She's goin' like a rocket!' gasped Willard, in admiration. 'Wow! Wish *I* could swim like that! She's some gran, isn't she?'

Super Gran reached the child, lifted her high out the water with one hand and swam – using only the other arm – towards the child's boat. And she *still* swam faster than most people could, with *both* arms!

'Take her home as fast as you can, before she gets her death of cold,' she told the other girls in the boat, as she handed the child in. 'And now,' she added, 'hold tight...!'

Before they knew what was happening, Super Gran had swum to the back of the girls' boat and, putting one hand on it and swimming with the other, she pushed the boat at speed back to the landing-stage!

When they reached it and the children stepped out, the boatman shouted: 'Hey – you there!' But Super Gran didn't wait to hear any more. She turned and swam back to Edison and Willard.

'That was terrific, Gran!' Willard greeted her, helping her aboard. 'Maybe you'll get a medal for that!'

'I should think so!' Edison agreed. 'What did the man say?'

'Don't know, lassie. Didn't wait to find out.'

'Thought you said you couldn't swim, Gran? ' Willard said.

'I told you – I couldn't...before! But I can do *any*-thing now! Didn't I tell you?'

She was all for rowing them a couple of times round the island in the middle of the lake, but Edison had other, more sensible, ideas.

'You'll do no such thing!' she said, a determined look on her face. 'You'll go straight home and change out of those wet clothes! At once!'

'Humph! Spoilsport!' Super Gran muttered as she rowed the boat back to the landing-stage. 'Och. A wee bit of water'll not hurt me!'

But Edison was very determined, when she had to be. 'It will, Super Gran. You could get pneumonia, or something. Besides, you've had enough excitement for one day, with the Super-ray and all your football and racing and swimming and everything. And we don't know if your Super-powers will last, or not. Dad said he didn't know if they would....'

Before Edison had a chance to explain further about the Super-machine and her dad, they had reached the pier.

The boatman stood goggle-eyed. He was surrounded by the crowd which had gathered on the landing-stage and on either side of it, round the sides of the lake, to welcome Super Gran ashore. For everyone on the banks of the lake had seen the rescue and now stood gazing, and cheering, as Super Gran rowed ashore, and landed.

'What's everybody standing about for?' Super Gran asked. 'Are they queueing up for boats? And who are they shouting at?'

'Don't be daft, Gran,' Willard grinned hugely, 'they're givin' you a big welcome. You're a hero!'

'A heroine, you mean,' Edison corrected him.

'A heroine? But why?' Super Gran asked.

'For saving the little girl, of course,' Edison explained.

'Och! That was nothing!'

The boatman tied the boat's rope to a ring on the landing-stage and then turned to glare at Super Gran in his best sour-faced manner.

'He's goin' to give you a life-savin' medal,' Willard smiled.

But he wasn't! Far from it!

'Oh, so you've decided to come out now, have you? After your little dip in the lake? Your little *illegal* dip!' He took a notebook and pencil from his pocket and started to write. 'Name?' he demanded.

'Super Gran,' replied Super Gran.

'Eh? What...?'

'She's super, isn't she?' Willard beamed, proudly. 'Did you see her go zoomin' through the water like a rocket...?'

'I did!' the man snapped. 'Swimming's not allowed! Not here! I want her name and address...!'

'But she wasn't swimming,' Edison chipped in. 'She went in to rescue that little girl who fell in. You must've seen her?'

'That's as may be. Swimming's not allowed in the boating-lake,' he glowered. 'Not in the *boating*-lake, see! You go to the *swimming* pool to swim, see? And pay! Not in here, for nothing. See?' He pointed to the notice-board nearby, which read: 'No Swimming Allowed'.

'Och! Come on, kids,' Super Gran muttered, as she went to push her way through the crowds. 'Never mind that scunnery-lugs! Let's go home.'

But that was easier said than done! For everyone in the crowd wanted to shake Super Gran's hand, slap her back and congratulate her. Everyone, that is, but the boatman!

'Hey! Hold on! Wait!' he yelled at them. 'I haven't got your name and address yet…!'

Super Gran looked back at him. 'I *told* you – I'm Super Gran!'

'No…hey…wait!' the boatman shouted again, but someone in the crowd decided to lend a hand – by pushing him off the landing-stage into the water.

'Help!' he gurgled, as his notebook and pencil floated away, 'I can't swim…!'

'Serves you right!' a woman told him, laughing. 'Super Gran could save you…but it's not allowed, is it?'

As the crowd roared with laughter, the boatman struggled, spluttering, to his feet and found that, just there, the water was shallow and only came up to his knees!

Meanwhile, Super Gran, Willard and Edison – complete with Super Gran's coat and trolley – managed to force their way through the crowd, to set off across the park to the exit.

'Let's run,' Super Gran suggested. 'It'll help to dry out my wet clothes.'

Willard, eager as ever, set off alongside her. But Edison groaned and, as usual, tripped – over a 'Keep Off the Grass' sign – and went sprawling. Why was someone always trying to make her run places; she had no desire to run places!

Super Gran stopped, came back and picked her up. 'Come on, I'll give you a piggy-back!'

'Put me down, Super Gran!' Edison exclaimed.

'You're an old lady! You'll hurt yourself!'

'Hurt myself? Blethers, lassie. Have you forgotten who I am? I keep telling you – I'm Super Gran! And I can do *any*thing!'

'There's no stopping you, is there?' Edison smiled.

'And I won't be needing those things again,' Super Gran added, as she placed her warm, winter coat on her shopping-trolley...and pushed it back down the slope towards the boating-lake!

4 Mrs Bottomly's Story

Willard, excited about his gran's new Super-powers, went home to tea and tried to tell his parents all about her. Without success!

His mother, as usual, just didn't believe him. She was too used to his coming home with fabulous tales of his imaginary exploits.

'Your gran playing football? Willard! Not again! Not some more of your stories! How often have I to tell you about fibs?'

'But Mum, I'm not…' he protested. 'It's true. She….'

'Nonsense! Whoever heard of such a thing!'

'Honest, Mum.' He took a deep breath, a very deep breath, and said: 'There was this Super-ray which shot out and hit Gran and made her Super and there was this girl who's always tripping over her big feet and she said something about her father and an Inventor and she played football Gran did and rowed a boat and rescued a little girl in the lake and….'

He said it all in the one breath, hoping to convince his mother before she interrupted him. But she wasn't going to be convinced.

'That's enough, Willard. I've got to get the tea ready….'

He wandered off to tell his father about his super Super Gran, but he was too busy to listen to him. His dad was the secretary of his works Golf Club and was busy arranging a team for a match.

'Mmm? What's that, son? About Gran? Oh, can you tell me later. I've got to 'phone one of our players. Our best player, in fact. Okay? Tell me later?'

Willard shrugged and wandered off again. No one would listen to him, but he was used to that. They'd hear all about Super Gran once everyone started talking about her and the Super things she could do; like the football and the swimming and everything. Once her adventures appeared in the newspapers and on the telly. *Then* maybe they'd believe him....

Next day, the Inventor told Tub that the machine was ready once more to turn him into a Superman, or, at least, a Super-Tub.

'But...ah...er...I don't think I should, boss,' Tub said, between mouthfuls of chocolate bar, playing for time until he could think up a suitable excuse for not being made Super at all. 'Ah...um...I've got a cold.' He sniffed. 'Yeah, that's it – me cold's worse, and it's bad to turn people into Super-people when they've got bad colds....'

'Nonsense! What's that got to do with it?' the Inventor snorted. 'Come on now, stand over against the wall, in front of the machine. I'll aim properly this time. I'll make sure Einstein doesn't move it. Are you ready?'

Tub ambled over to the wall. 'But boss....' He racked his brains to come up with a good excuse, in vain.

But then, just as the Inventor was about to operate

the machine, Tub was saved – by Mrs Bottomly, the housekeeper.

She knocked on the door and the Inventor automatically yelled:

'Go away! We're busy!'

But that didn't stop her. It usually took more than that to stop Mrs Bottomly. She opened the door, popped her head round it and addressed the Inventor: 'Hey, Professor....'

'Go away!' he repeated, more loudly. 'And I'm not a professor,' he added, although, to be honest, he was secretly quite pleased to be called 'Professor'. It made him feel important. 'Well? What is it? I'm busy!'

'There ain't none fish left,' Mrs Bottomly said, with a frown.

The Inventor tut-tutted. 'That's not correct, Mrs Bottomly.'

'It is, you know! The fishmonger's sold out!'

'No, no, no! I meant: there *isn't any* fish left. Not: there *ain't none*....'

'That's what I *said*!' Mrs Bottomly replied, indignantly. 'There ain't none fish left! So what'll I make for your lunch?'

'Oh, how should *I* know!' the Inventor snapped, irritably. 'There are plenty of other things. Now – go away and let me get on with my experiment.'

'But there ain't none meat neither,' the housekeeper continued, 'not in the house, anyways....'

'Oh well, don't bother *me* about it, Mrs Bottomly, there's a good chap. I mean...there's a good...ah ...um....'

'I suppose I could boil a couple o' eggs…' she began, thoughtfully.

'Oh, go and boil your head…!' the Inventor muttered.

'Wot was that? Eh?' The woman glared.

'Ah…um…I said…er, go and boil your eggs. That's it. Good idea. Or omelettes. Or cheese sandwiches. Or something. *Any*thing! Just so long as you get out of here and leave us alone!'

He walked towards her and started to close the door, carefully – but firmly – pushing her out of the room. But Mrs Bottomly decided to take an interest in the Inventor's goings-on.

'Here, Professor – wot you doin' anyways?' she asked.

'I told you. It's an experiment. And now….' He tried again to push her out.

'An' wot's old wot's–'is–name doin' standin' there, lookin' so miserable for?' She pushed the door open again, edging herself back inside. She pointed at Tub. 'I mean, the fat boy?'

'I'm not fat, it's muscles!' Tub scowled. 'And he's trying to turn me into a Superman, that's what he's trying to do,' he yelled across to her. 'And I don't want to be a Superman, or a Super-anything. Not now. But he won't listen! I'm quite happy *not* being a Superman. If I can just go on learning my judo and karate and wrestling and kung-fu and….'

The Inventor hissed at him: 'Shhhh! Don't tell the whole world!' He didn't want the world to know, yet, that he was about to conquer it and start ruling it; the

41

world would find out in due course!

But Tub just ignored him. If he could only get Mrs Bottomly interested in his plight she might, somehow, be able to rescue him from the Inventor, and his rotten Super-machine. 'And he wants me to help him to rule the world,' he blurted out, ignoring the Inventor's plea for silence. 'Whatever that means!'

'Yes...well, anyway...ah....' The Inventor cleared his throat, noisily, to drown Tub's words, and he turned back towards the door, meaning to close it on his housekeeper, to lock her outside the room. But he was too late. He'd taken his eyes off her for a second, and she'd taken the chance to slip inside.

She dodged past the Inventor, and over to Tub. 'A Superman? Wot d'you mean – a Superman? Wot's a Superman? Eh? Tell me!'

Tub shrugged. 'How should I know? I don't know. Ask him! He hasn't made me into one yet. And I don't want him to!'

Mrs Bottomly swung round, suddenly, on her boss. 'Here!' she said. 'Wot's a Superman? Eh?'

'Never you mind!' the Inventor snapped, taking her arm to try to lead her towards the door again.

'I think,' Tub chipped in, 'it's someone who's got a lot of strength and...and...well, Super-human powers, or something.'

'Oh!' Mrs Bottomly's face lit up with sudden understanding. 'Oh, I know wot you mean! You mean like Super *Gran?* Is that it? Only a Super*man* instead? Eh?'

There was a sudden silence in the room, as Tub and the Inventor looked at each other. Then:

'Who?' said the Inventor. 'Super-who?'

'Super Gran,' Mrs Bottomly repeated. 'I told you.'

'Super *Gran*? *Super* Gran?' murmured the Inventor, over and over.

He wondered if Edison's father had, after all, managed to make someone else Super before he, the Inventor, had been able to pinch the machine. And then he wondered if Mr Black possibly had a *second* machine; one that the Inventor hadn't known about.

'What...what are you talking about, Mrs Bottomly?' he asked. 'You're not serious, are you?' He began to laugh, trying to pass the whole thing off as a joke. 'A Super *Gran*, did you say? Ha, ha!'

'Yes, Professor, you 'eard!' Mrs Bottomly said. 'I was at the fish shop this morning, on my way 'ere. Remember? I told you. There ain't none fish....'

'Yes, yes, yes! Don't start that again!'

'Well, anyways,' Mrs Bottomly continued, 'a little kiddy's ball rolls under a motor car, in the 'igh Street, an' 'e tries to get it out, like. But, of course, 'e can't, can 'e? An' then this little ol' lady comes along, sees wot 'e's up to an' – calm as you like! – she lifts up that there car...with one 'and, mind you!...and lets the little nipper walk right under it to get 'is ball out.' She laughed. 'Just as well the driver wasn't in it at the time, eh? 'E'd be sea-sick!'

'Oh, come now...!' the Inventor began, not knowing whether to believe the woman's story or not.

But Mrs Bottomly wasn't finished yet. 'Oh, and when someone says wot a feat o' strength that was and wot does she call 'erself– "Mrs Samson"? – laughin' like, the old lady says no, 'er name is Super Gran.'

'Super Gran?' the Inventor murmured thoughtfully. 'Mmm….'

'Bo–oss…' Tub said, slowly – and equally thoughtfully. 'Yesterday…in the park….' Tub had had *another* brilliant thought. That was two in two days, a record!

'Yes, that's what *I* was thinking, Tub,' the Inventor agreed. 'I wonder…?' He turned to Mrs Bottomly again. 'What's her name, do you know?'

'I *told* you, why don't you listen!' the woman replied, stamping her foot, impatiently. 'She said it was Super Gr….'

Her boss glared at her. 'I mean – what's her *real* name?'

'*I* dunno,' the woman snapped, beginning to tire of the whole thing. She wanted to get on with making the lunch. 'Ow should *I* know? I've never seen 'er before, 'ave I?'

'She was down in the High Street?' he asked.

Mrs Bottomly nodded as the Inventor ushered her out of the room; and this time she went without a fuss.

The Inventor switched the machine off.

'You're not going on with the experiment?' Tub beamed.

'No, I'm not going on with it…' the Inventor began, as Tub stepped away from the wall, relieved, and unwrapped another chocolate bar to celebrate. He munched it happily.

'I'm not going on with it,' the Inventor repeated, adding: 'just yet! First – I want you to go down to the

High Street....'

'Oh yes?'

'And find this Super Gran....'

'Huh?'

'Find out where she lives. I want to know if the Super-ray struck her in the park yesterday, and made her act like this. Or she may always have been strong. I'll have to find out.'

He ushered Tub out of the door. 'And if it *was* Black's ray...er...that is, *my* ray which did it, I'll have to switch it over to the reversing one.'

Tub looked puzzled. 'Reversing one? What for?'

'To change her back to normal again, dumb-head!' the Inventor explained. 'We can't have just *any* old, ordinary member of the public running about being Super, with Super-powers. Especially a little old lady!'

He took Tub to the front door and pushed him outside. 'You know what to do. Go straight down to the High Street and find this old Super Gran woman. Right?'

So Tub, not really knowing what he was supposed to be doing, or who exactly he was looking for, took the bus into town, to the High Street. All he knew was: it was a little old lady – and she could lift motor cars!

He loitered about outside the shops, until a policeman eyed him with suspicion; so he thought he'd better go inside some of them. But once inside, the shop assistants eyed him with suspicion, thinking he was a thief; so Tub had to go back outside again. He couldn't win!

He wandered up and down the street and round a

couple of corners, aimlessly, hoping that some little old lady would come along, lift another motor car and reveal herself as Super Gran! It was hopeless. And pointless, just hanging about, waiting. And boring. And it made him feel hungry, again!

After a while, he leaned against a bus stop – which didn't look quite so suspicious – took out his latest paperback, entitled: *Self-Defence For Beginners*, and had a read at it.

He smiled to himself as he thought of all the things he could do to the Inventor and all the others who pushed him around and said he was fat, once he'd mastered all the fighting skills outlined in the book. Then he thought of all the things he could do if he were a Super-Tub, and he wondered again if, after all, it mightn't be a bad thing to be Super.

While Tub was day-dreaming a little old lady approached him, with two children – a boy and a girl.

'Let's play leap-frog,' the old lady said, and promptly leapt over a parking-meter!

'Oh, you old show-off!' the girl laughed.

'Wonder what time it is?' the boy said, as they passed Tub. 'Isn't it lunch-time yet? I'm starvin'!'

'I'll soon tell you, from the Town Hall clock,' replied the old woman, who was barely an inch taller than her young companions.

'But you can't *see* the Town Hall clock from here,' the girl said, pointing to a high wall across the road, with posters all over it. 'It's behind that wall over there!'

Tub saw the little old lady put her hands up to her

temples and stare hard at the wall for a few seconds.
'No?' she said. 'Well, it's just gone twelve o'clock,
lassie. So there!'

'But...but how do you know that?' the girl asked.

'Easy-peasy!' the old woman grinned. 'I can see
through walls!'

'Wow! Cr–rumbs!' the boy exclaimed. 'Imagine
that!'

'As well as everything else!' the girl said, impressed.

A bus drew up at the stop, just then, and Tub
boarded it, not realizing that he had let Super Gran slip
through his fingers....

5 Edison's Story

'Well?' the Inventor asked, when Tub returned. 'How did you get on? Did you find her? What's her name? Where does she live?'

Tub threw himself into the workshop's one and only chair, which almost collapsed under his weight. He was tired out with all his tramping up and down the High Street, and in and out of shops.

'I didn't. No. Don't know. Don't know!' Tub said, in answer to the Inventor's four questions. 'And I've just about worn me feet out to me ankle-bones with all that walking about. *And* I'm famished! It's past me lunch-time!'

'Never mind all that. Did you find her?'

'I told you – no, I didn't.'

'Then what did you come back for?' The Inventor was indignant.

'For me lunch. I told you – I'm starving!' He only wanted *his* share of the meal Mrs Bottomly would have prepared for them.

'I meant you to stay out until you found her,' the Inventor explained. He licked his lips. 'I had a lovely double cheese omelette. Delicious!'

Tub was livid. 'You rotter! Half of that *double* was my *single* cheese omelette! You've had *my* share!'

'Well, you weren't here, were you?' the Inventor

replied.

Tub was mad and he tried to summon up all his courage to give his boss a chop...a karate chop! But he couldn't. He wouldn't have had any more success than he'd had with his little sister! And besides, he still had his back-pay to come, if he behaved himself. So he decided to keep his temper – meantime!

'You didn't say that!' he protested. 'And you didn't give me money for a lunch. So I thought I'd come back here....'

The Inventor grumbled, muttering, as he took a couple of coins out of his purse and tossed them to Tub. 'Here, take this. Buy yourself a packet of crisps, or something. And now, off you go and have another look for that old woman....'

'Huh!' Tub snorted, huffed. 'Well, I *did* see an old woman, if you must know....'

'What...?' the Inventor barked, suddenly interested.

'Yeah, but don't panic,' Tub assured him. 'Don't panic. She wasn't the one. She couldn't lift cars and things. At least,' he added, thoughtfully, 'I didn't see her lifting any.'

'Oh, and what could *she* do?' the Inventor asked, sarcastically. 'What was *her* speciality? Punching holes in walls? Eh?' He roared with laughter at his own joke.

'No,' Tub replied, innocently, 'but she could *see* through them. *And* she played leap-frog over a parking-meter!'

'What...!' the Inventor thundered.

'So she said, anyway. Said she could tell the time through a solid brick wall. I was waiting for the bus, and....'

'An old lady leaping over a parking-meter?' The Inventor was speechless. 'And seeing through walls?' He turned crimson.

Tub related the conversation he'd overheard, to the Inventor.'Have you ever heard anything so daft?' he laughed. 'Telling the time through a wall!'

The Inventor had been using a spanner as Tub had been talking, and now he dropped it – with shock. It hit his toe and bounced off with a clatter on to the floor. He yelped in pain.

'An...an old woman with...with two children?' he spluttered.'An old woman?' he repeated. 'And two children?' Tub nodded. 'A boy and a girl?' Tub nodded again.

'In the park, yesterday,' the Inventor whispered, slowly, so that it would sink into even *Tub's* brain, 'there was an old woman...with a boy and a girl...remember?' He turned purple. 'The Super-ray...that's who it hit!'

'Huh?' Tub grunted.

'You saw her this morning and you let her go!' he roared at Tub. 'You great spotted idiot, you!'

'But...but, boss,' Tub protested, 'you told me to look for a *strong* old lady – not one who could jump over parking-meters and see through walls!'

The Inventor picked up the fallen spanner and was strongly tempted to bounce it off Tub's nut. 'It was a Super Gran you were looking for. A *Super* Gran. That's a little old granny who can do Super things...like lifting cars, jumping meters, seeing through walls!

They're Super things, ain't they…er…aren't they?'

'I – I suppose so,' Tub agreed, now it was pointed out to him.

'Grrrr!' The Inventor gnashed his teeth, angrily. 'Get out there. Find her again. Don't let her out of your sight. Follow her!'

'But, boss….'

'Right?' the Inventor roared. He pointed to the door, like a football referee ordering a player off the field. 'Go!' He pushed the unwilling – and still starving! – Tub out of the house once more, on his errand.

'Humph! It's all right for him,' Tub muttered as he slowly wandered down the street, in search of a bus. 'He's had *his* lunch – and *my* lunch…and all *I* get's a rotten packet of crisps! Huh! Big deal!'

He boarded a bus, muttering to himself all the way into town: 'Huh! I'm just wasting me time, that's all I'm doing. Just wasting me time….'

Meanwhile, Super Gran, Willard and Edison had been having a snack lunch in a café. And this gave Edison the chance, at long last, to explain all about the Super-machine.

'You see,' she told them, 'my dad's an inventor – that's why my names are Edison and Faraday! – and he invented two or three little inventions, which this rotten Inventor pinched. To sell, to make money off them. But this time it wasn't a little invention – it was a big one. A good invention. A *great* invention. The Super-machine. Which was supposed to make wheat and vegetables and things grow large and grow quickly, to solve the food shortage. But, instead, it made Super Gran Super, didn't it?'

'But who *is* this Inventor scunner?' Super Gran asked.

'He's a man my dad used to work for, at one time,' Edison explained, 'but his inventions were no good, useless, so he started nicking Dad's instead. And Dad's an invalid now, too! Got injured in a car accident.'

'And this Inventor stole the Super-machine?' Super Gran said.

'Yes. After our budgie became Super.'

'Your budgie?' Willard spluttered over a drink.

Edison nodded. 'Our budgie, Chico, got in the way of the ray from the machine – and became Super!'

'A Super-budgie?' Willard said, hardly able to believe it. 'What happened? Where is it? You could take it to a zoo!'

Edison shook her head, and grinned. 'He burst out of his cage with his Super-strength, and flew away...with next door's cat!'

Willard and his gran laughed at the idea of a tiny Super-budgie carrying a heavy cat in its little tiny claws, and flying away with it.

'Anyway,' Edison continued, 'this so-called Inventor – thief is more like it – sent his gang over to steal the machine one night, after dark.'

'His gang?' Super Gran said. 'He's got a gang, the midden?'

'He must have. It'd take three or four men to carry the machine, it's heavy. And we heard a lorry driving away, through the night. And Dad won't go to the police about it. Says he'll easily build another one. But that takes money, and we haven't got any.'

She sighed, then continued: 'Anyway, I suspected the Inventor, and I traced him to one of those big houses near the park. And that's when I met you, yesterday.'

'Don't you worry, lassie,' Super Gran assured her, 'I'll help you to find this scunner of an Inventor. Me and my Super-powers! You see, I can do....'

'Anything?' Edison smiled.

'Right first time!'

'Dad doesn't bother about getting his inventions pinched. He's too easy-going. But *I* mind!' She flushed, angrily. '*I'm* going to get his machine back, *and* I'll get the police on to him!'

Super Gran could see that Edison could be very determined and was only too willing to help her. She stood up. 'Come on, drink up, Willie. Let's get after the wee bachle.'

The old lady was all for *running* back to the park from town, in search of the Inventor, but Edison persuaded her to take a bus instead. For one thing, Super Gran might use up all her Super-energy, and not have enough left to tackle the Inventor with. And for another thing, Edison would never have been able to keep up with her!

'Let's go upstairs,' Super Gran grinned, as they boarded a bus. 'I've not been able to go upstairs on a bus for years and years.' And she leapt up the stairs, *two* at a time!

'Yah! Show-off!' Edison laughed, as she and Willard

followed her up *one* at a time.

'Wonder how many Super-powers you've got, Gran?' Willard said, when they had sat down. 'You've got Super-strength, Super-speed, Super-swimming....'

'Super-hearing...' added Super Gran.

'And Super-sight, now,' said Edison. 'Sort of X-ray eyesight. Terrific, isn't it?'

'Have you anything *else* Super?' Willard asked.

'Don't know. I haven't tried everything – yet! Give me a chance!' Super Gran chuckled. 'Maybe the lassie knows what else I'm likely to do?' She turned to Edison, who shrugged.

'Not really. You see, Chico, the Super-budgie, flew away before Dad could test all its Super-powers.' She smiled as she gazed out of the bus window. 'Just think, out there, somewhere, there's a Super-budgie on the loose....'

'Picking up great big pussy cats, and things!' Super Gran laughed.

'Can you really see through walls, Gran?' Willard asked. 'Or were you just having us on?'

'Of *course* I can see through walls, Willie,' Super Gran retorted, indignantly. 'I told you – *I* can do....'

'Anything!' the other two added, together, laughing.

'Go on then, Gran,' Willard challenged her, 'tell us what's goin' on inside that building out there.' He pointed out of the window towards a building at a corner of the High Street.

All that could be seen from the bus was a plain brick wall. The windows had frosted glass through which nothing could be seen, and there was no ordinary way of seeing inside the building.

'But that's spying!' Super Gran protested.

'Go on,' Willard teased, 'you *were* only kiddin' us, Gran, weren't you? It was just a trick, wasn't it?'

'Jings, laddie! It was *not* a trick!' Super Gran almost stamped her foot, indignantly, at not being believed. 'I'll show you....'

She stared at the building, her hands pressed to her head, as the bus stopped at a stop.

It suddenly lurched forward again and, as it did so, Super Gran gasped: 'Jings! That's awful!'

'What is?' Edison asked.

But Super Gran didn't reply. She merely jumped out of her seat, dived along the aisle and plunged down the stairs, two at a time, past the confused conductor!

Edison turned to Willard, puzzled. '*Now* what?'

'Dunno!' Willard shrugged.

'Come on then,' Edison cried, 'let's get after her!'

The conductor had just started to climb the stairs, calling out: 'Fares please!' but had then added: 'Ugh! Oof! Mind out!' as Super Gran collided with him, spinning him round on his feet, on the platform, and knocking the breath from him. 'Guh!' he yelped.

He watched her jumping off the bus – dangerously – and was just recovering and was starting to go up the stairs again, when Edison and Willard descended on him.

He shook his fist at them as they, also, jumped off the moving bus. 'Hey! That there's not allowed!'

Then he remembered: 'Hey! Your fares! You 'aven't

paid your fares! None o' you! Come back 'ere!'

As the bus continued down the street the conductor hung out of it, shaking his fist at them. Then he went to climb the stairs once more, looking carefully up them this time, in case some more fare-dodging daredevils were about to throw themselves at him. 'Huh!' he muttered. 'Some folks'll do anything to dodge payin' their fares!'

Edison and Willard, on the pavement, saw Super Gran zooming round the corner into the side street. As they hurried after her, Edison realized that the building which Super Gran's X-ray eyes had 'looked into' was a bank.

'Gran! Wait for me...er, us!' Willard called after her.

'What's wrong, Super Gran?' Edison shouted.

But Super Gran didn't look back. She raced round the corner towards the huge wooden door of the bank and she didn't stop! She ran straight at it and kung-fu kicked a large hole smack in the middle of it – with one foot!

6 The Bank Raid

Just as the Capitol Bank opened its doors after lunch, three bank-robbers with stocking-masks over their faces forced their way in and slammed the door shut behind them. Outside, in a getaway car, they left a fourth man, waiting for them. The leader stood in front of the counter, pointing a gun at the bank-staff, while, behind the counter, his two mates filled sacks with money from a large safe.

'Hurry up, Harry, Joe,' he urged, as he waved his gun towards the manager and his staff. 'Don't take all day....'

But that was about as far as the bank-robbers got!

Suddenly, there was a terrific bang from the front of the bank as the door shattered and Super Gran hurtled her way through the hole she'd made in it – making a sudden, and dramatic, entrance!

The leader swung his head round and his mouth gaped open, in amazement, when he saw that a little old lady was responsible for the big jagged hole in the door. It was a big enough shock to see *anyone* come hurtling through a hole kicked in a big, thick door, but a little old lady...whew!

But that was all the leader saw. For that was all he had time to see! Super Gran hit him once, before he could move or aim his gun at her, or do anything. He slumped to the floor and lay there, suddenly desiring a long, deep sleep!

Super Gran didn't stop. She leapt over the fallen crook and vaulted nimbly over the bank counter – steel grille and all! – and landed beside Harry and Joe, who'd stopped filling the sacks when they heard the door being shattered and saw their boss being battered! And now it was their turn!

Super Gran banged their heads together – as gently as she knew how to – although even that was too much for them! The crack echoed round the bank and the two men thudded to the floor, to join their boss in having forty winks!

'Jings! Is that the lot? That was easy-peasy!' Super Gran grinned, looking round the faces of the astonished bank-staff. 'You'd better send for the polis [she meant the police] to get them carted away,' she said, pointing to the crooks. And then she vaulted over the counter again, from a standing start!

The manager stepped forward, lowering his hands, having been told to 'stick 'em up'. He was speechless. 'But...but...but....'

It had all happened so quickly – twenty seconds and it was all over! – and he had never seen anything like it in his life before. No one had! 'But...but you're a little old lady....'

'Blethers! I am not! I'm Super Gran!' she exclaimed proudly, putting one foot, gently, she hoped, on the stomach of the robber leader as he lay on the floor.

Edison and Willard, following Super Gran, had seen the huge hole in the door and had scrambled through

it, to see what she was up to. They were standing a few feet inside the door and had seen the second part of Super Gran's action.

'Cr—crumbs!' Willard gasped. 'A bank raid....'

'Foiled by good old Super Gran!' Edison added.

'Not so much of the "old", if you don't mind!' Super Gran laughed, as she walked towards them.

'Is that what you saw from the bus, Gran? The bank raid?' Willard asked.

'Is *that* why you went dashing off like that?' Edison added.

Super Gran nodded. 'Aye, that's right. Lucky I've got X-ray eyesight, isn't it?'

The manager, following Super Gran to the door, blinked when he heard this. 'X-ray eyesight? What...?' He just couldn't believe it. But he'd seen for himself how she'd dealt with those crooks. The strength of the woman! And the speed! And the way she could jump! She was fantastic!

He looked round his staff to see if they too had seen what he had seen, or had he imagined it all? And his staff burst into applause! So they *had* seen it.

'She *is* Super, isn't she?' Edison beamed, as if answering the manager's unspoken thoughts. 'She's Super Gran.'

Super Gran flexed her muscles. 'And I can do *any-thing....*'

'But...but...you're an old lady!' The manager couldn't get over it.

'And it was my dad's machine that did it,' Edison told the man, proudly. 'Only it got stolen....'

That reminded them. The Inventor. They'd forgotten all about him in all the excitement.

'Come on, Willie, lassie,' Super Gran urged, 'let's get after that wee bachle!' She started towards the door, then stopped. 'Oh, and I'm sorry I made a mess of your door like that! I didn't stop to think!'

'Oh, that's all right,' the manager murmured, slowly. 'Any time!' He was too confused, just then, to say anything else.

Super Gran turned back to lead Edison and Willard out through the hole in the door and, as she bent down to creep through, she came face-to-face with Tub!

Tub, sitting looking out of the window of his bus, had seen Super Gran running at the bank door and kicking the hole in it. By the time he'd managed to jump off the bus and get back to the bank he was too late to see Super Gran's actual performance with the crooks. But he'd peeked in through the hole and had seen the result of Super Gran's work – the unconscious crooks' leader.

Tub had ducked back and then, on peeking through a second time, he'd come face-to-face with Super Gran. His first reaction was to turn and run for his life! Which, he found out, was a mistake!

For Super Gran, seeing him running, mistook him for another bank-robber. She leapt through the hole after him, yelling as she ran: 'Look! There's another baddie! Let's get him!'

Willard and Edison scrambled out through the hole after her, Willard shouting: 'Maybe that's their getaway man, Gran!'

'Well, he won't get away from me!' Super Gran bawled, in reply.

'Help! Stop!' gasped Tub, looking round to see Super Gran speeding after him, and getting closer. 'It's a mistake! I can explain!' The whole thing, he reckoned, was getting out of control.

Super Gran stretched out her hands towards Tub as he tried to explain: '*I'm* not a bank-robber. I'm....'

But she didn't let him finish. She threw herself forward in a flying rugby tackle, caught him round the ankles and brought him crashing to the ground.

'Gotcha, you scunner!' she cried, in triumph, as she landed, somehow, on top of him.

As they lay there in the street, like a couple of television wrestlers, grappling together, Tub managed to get one arm free, to point with. And he pointed at a car, parked outside the bank, which was now starting to move off.

'*I* was only watching you,' Tub gasped, from somewhere beneath Super Gran. 'There's the *real* getaway man – and he's getting away now. Stop *him*!'

Tub was annoyed. After all the time he'd spent studying self-defence this was his chance to have used it. He should have stopped and faced up to the little old lady. But then he remembered that she wasn't an *ordinary* little old lady, as the bank-robbers had already discovered, to their cost!

Super Gran, for her part, hadn't quite heard what Tub had said, for she was half-smothering him at the time. But she saw the car zooming past them, and she saw its driver sticking his head out of the window, muttering: 'Cor blimey! I'm off!'

The getaway man couldn't understand what had happened to his mates and he'd been wondering what to do. His orders were: to sit in the car, with the engine running, outside the bank, until the robbers came out with the cash. But he'd seen Super Gran bursting her way in through the door and, minutes later, diving out again, to chase Tub, who wasn't one of the gang! He'd wondered what was happening, but now, seeing Tub pointing towards *him*, he'd decided to scarper, mates or no mates!

As the man saw Super Gran leaping to her feet, in his mirror, he put his foot on the accelerator. He'd already seen Super Gran's Super-strength and Super-speed and he wanted to sample neither of them, thank you very much!

'He's getting away!' Edison cried.

'Not for long, he won't, lassie! I'll get him!' Super Gran promised, as she sped after the car.

'If he stops at the traffic-lights you'll get him.'

'Traffic-lights?' Willard exclaimed. 'Huh! Gran doesn't need traffic-lights!'

And he was right. She didn't! She caught up with the car after only a few dozen yards, and she put her hand on the handle of the driver's door. She held on, and pulled…and pulled it right off the car!

The driver, amazed at seeing the door suddenly disappearing, panicked, turned the steering-wheel the wrong way – and crashed the car into a lamp-post.

By now the High Street was full of people, and pandemonium!

A passing police panda-car arrived, to take charge of the bank-robbers; shoppers and shop assistants crowded round to see what was going on; the traffic had come to a standstill; a crowd gathered round the crashed car; the bank manager was fighting his way through the mob to reach Super Gran, to tell her she'd get a big reward; a reporter from the local newspaper, *The Chisleton Comet*, was asking everyone questions; and a press photographer was photographing every-one in sight!

Finally, a police-sergeant managed to get hold of Super Gran, to question her about the whole affair, the reporter writing her answers into his notebook, the bank manager hovering in the background.

'Are you *sure* you did the things the manager said you did?' the sergeant asked her, scratching his head with his pencil, as the manager nodded his head violently.

'I mean,' the sergeant went on, 'he says you clobbered all those crooks by yourself! Four of them? *And* bashed that dirty big hole in his door? *And* yanked the door off that car?' He sniggered. 'I mean, you *couldn't* have! Nobody could! Never mind a little old lady like you!'

'Of course I did! Jings, Sergeant! Who else *could* have done it? Who *else* but Super Gran? That's me, you see? I keep telling everybody – I can do....'

'*Any*thing!' Edison and Willard yelled out, in chorus, from somewhere among the crowd.

'Precisely!' She bent down. 'Look – I'll show you!' She grasped the police-sergeant's ankles and lifted the man, who was six feet tall and must have weighed sixteen stones, right into the air, above her head. 'See?'

'Hey! Here! Put me down!' the sergeant gasped, in terror. 'Put me down at once!' He dropped his pencil and notebook in his surprise.

The crowd clapped, cheered, whistled and shouted comments:

'Hey missus – put him down. You don't know where he's been!'

'Hey missus – pick somebody you own size!'

'Look – it takes a little old lady to uphold the law!'

And Super Gran, grinning at the crowd's applause, curtsied, still holding the policeman aloft! But then, seeing that he was rapidly turning purple with anger and embarrassment, she lowered him gently to the ground and dived away quickly into the crowd before he could arrest her for making a fool of him in public like that.

'Come on, Willie, lassie – let's go!' she yelled, as the children slipped through the crowd and followed her.

'Come back here!' the sergeant shouted after them, shaking his ham-sized fist at them. But they didn't look back.

They ran along the street, turned a corner, glanced back, to see that they weren't being chased, and slowed down, much to Edison's relief.

'Here's a bus coming,' she pointed, gasping. '*Now* maybe we can get after that rotten Inventor, eh?'

7 The Inventor Makes Plans

The Inventor had wasted enough time. He decided to find out Super Gran's address by some other means. He couldn't rely on Tub. Tub was hopeless.

He shuddered at the thought of making Tub into a Super-Tub, and turning him loose to help him rule the world. He could see now that it would be a mistake. Tub would never be any good to him, Super or otherwise!

The Inventor had schemed and dreamed for years of becoming the ruler of the world and he knew that the fantastic Super-machine was the very thing to help him on his way; it would give him power. He could foresee a whole army of Supermen, all doing what *he* wanted. No one would be able to stop him; he'd take over Britain, then Europe, America, Russia, China ...the world! He could do as he liked, say what he pleased, make everyone toe the line and do what *he* wanted them to do.

The first step was going to have been making Tub Super – just to see if it worked! And then, if it did, he'd have made himself Super. And then, his army of Super-soldiers! Nobody and nothing could stop him....

But now that this Super Gran person had proved that the machine *did* work, it was just a matter of making her normal again and making someone else –

not Tub – Super in her place.

No, he thought, Tub was too soft to be a Superman. He wanted a hard, tough person – someone like Benny, for example. Now *there* was a tough guy, if ever he'd met one. *And* his boys. Benny and his boys – his gang – were proper toughies. In fact, the Inventor always thought of the three toughies as 'The Toughies'. And, as he'd never been told their names, the Inventor had secretly christened them 'Rough', 'Tough' and 'Gruff'!

It had been Benny and the Toughies who had pinched the Super-machine from Edison's dad for the Inventor, in the first place. And they'd be ideal, thought the Inventor, as he rubbed his hands together in glee, to start off his Super-army.

But first things first. He still had to find Super Gran and make her normal again, as soon as possible. For until he did, he wouldn't be the only person in the world with Super-powers and that wouldn't do!

He went to his telephone and dialled the local newspaper.

'Hello,' a young girl's voice answered him. '*Chisleton Comet*, Editorial Department. Can I help you?'

'Ah! Yes…um…good afternoon,' the Inventor began, trying to be as charming as he possibly could be. 'You may have heard of the little old lady in town who goes round lifting up cars and things…?' He knew it sounded ridiculous, but he had to say it anyway.

The girl interrupted him. 'Oh yes, I've heard about her. She foiled a bank raid and made a hole in a door and she made a car crash and…and things….'

'Oh…?' The Inventor, who hadn't yet heard about Super Gran's latest exploits, was a bit taken aback. But he went on: 'Oh…ah…yes, is that so? Anyways…I mean, anyway…you'll know where she lives, won't you?'

'Who shall I say is asking?' the girl asked.

'Oh…ah…my name's Amerson,' the Inventor lied. 'You know – the…ah…famous television producer…?'

'Oh? Mr Amerson?' The girl's voice brightened considerably. He *must* be important, she thought, if he's on the telly. *Everyone* on the telly is important! 'Yes, Mr Amerson?'

'Yes…ah…I want to make a…ah…ah…TV programme about this wonderful old lady. Trouble is, I don't know where to contact her. Don't know her address.'

'Hold on….' The girl went away for a few seconds, and returned, to say: 'She lives at 23 Highview Road, Mr Amerson….' The girl had by now put on her best, politest, most polished voice, hoping to impress 'Mr Amerson', who'd be sure to get her onto the telly in one of his shows.

The Inventor thanked the girl, promised that her newspaper would get a mention on his TV programme and put the 'phone down. Then he went back to the Super-machine to make sure that it would work in reverse, ready to make Super Gran normal again.

Let Super Gran have as much fame and publicity as she liked, just now, he thought, as he removed a panel from the machine, to adjust the controls and the wiring. After he'd made her normal again no one would bother with her any more; not the newspapers, nor anyone else. In fact, no one would believe then that it had all really happened to her. The eye witnesses to her many exploits would begin to think they had only imagined them all!

That is, until the Super-Inventor with his Super-army of Super-Toughies took over the world. *Then* they would know, all right. But they wouldn't know...what had hit them!

Just then Tub, still famished (one small packet of crisps wasn't nearly enough to satisfy a growing lad like Tub for five minutes), returned to the Inventor's house. He explained how he had tangled with Super Gran outside the bank, but that he'd lost her in the crowd.

'I used me judo and karate on her,' he lied, 'and I really had her tied up in knots, but....' He stopped. The Inventor had raised one eyebrow, in disbelief; he knew better than that.

Tub tried to add to his explanation, but the Inventor didn't seem to be interested. And he wondered why the Inventor wasn't madder than he was at him not being able to find out Super Gran's address.

'She lives at 23 Highview Road,' the Inventor told him, when Tub mentioned it to him. 'I found out from the local newspaper. I 'phoned them.'

'Huh?' Tub snorted, indignantly. 'After all the trouble I went to, too....'

'Shut up, Tub. You're beginning to sound like a train; to too...to too....' He laughed at his own joke, pleased now that things were beginning to go his way, at last.

Tub, not understanding the joke, was puzzled.

'So I've got her now,' the Inventor gloated. 'I know her address. I can pick her up any time I want to!'

'Huh!' Tub retorted. 'It's more like *her* picking *you* up any time *she* wants to! Anyway, what're you going to do with her once you've got her?'

'Don't worry, Tub. I won't do her any harm,' the Inventor assured him, cheerfully, and confidently.

'You're not kidding, you won't!' Tub murmured, under his breath.

'I'll just put her in front of the machine and normalize her.'

'You'll what?' Tub asked. 'You'll marmalize her?'

'Normalize. Make her normal. Take away her Super-powers.'

'Oh yes?' Tub smiled, sort of inwardly. He knew better! He knew Super Gran better than the Inventor knew her.

'Yes. But don't worry, I won't hurt her.'

Tub snorted. 'Humph! That's a good one! *You* won't hurt *her*? What about *her* hurting *you*?'

'Oh-oh, maybe you're right,' the Inventor admitted, rubbing his chin, thoughtfully. 'I was forgetting about her Super-strength.'

'Yeah, and her Super-everything-else!' Tub muttered, rubbing some of his bruises.

The Inventor was deep in thought. 'Mmm, let's see – we'd better take some ropes with us, to tie her up with. And a net. Just in case. Better still, we'll take chains! *That* should do the trick. She won't be able to break out of chains, will she?'

'I wouldn't bet on it...hey! Wha–wha–what d'you mean "we"?' Tub backed away from the Inventor. 'I–I–I'm not going to fetch her.' The very idea was enough to make Tub extremely nervous! 'I've had enough of her!'

'What about all that judo and karate you were telling me about?' his boss teased. 'What about all those knots you were tying her up in?'

'You can fetch her by yourself....'

The Inventor opened his mouth, to argue with Tub, and insist that he should go with him, but then he thought better of it. After all, Tub was no use. Benny was. He'd get Benny and the Toughies to help him fetch Super Gran. Surely he – the Inventor – Benny and three Toughies would be more than a match for one little old lady!

The Inventor 'phoned Benny, to tell him to come over right away, but Benny was out of town (doing some shoplifting!) so he left a message, telling him to come over first thing in the morning...and to bring his gang with him!

While his boss was busy on the 'phone, Tub took the chance to sneak away and raid the larder, to satisfy his rumbling tummy, which was now thundering away like mad!

Meanwhile, Super Gran, on her way to the park in the bus, with Edison and Willard, was having second thoughts about going in search of the Inventor.

'You don't mean you're *not* going to find the Inventor, after all?' cried Edison, horrified. After all the delays caused by bank raids, chasing Tub, wrecking cars and lifting policemen, surely Super Gran wasn't going to disappoint her by *not* helping to find the Inventor and getting the Super-machine back to her dad? Surely Edison wasn't going to have to start searching for him on her own again? And without the help of Super Gran's Super-powers, too?

'Don't panic, lassie,' Super Gran assured her, cheerily. 'I didn't mean I wasn't going to look for your Inventor. I thought I'd collect all my old friends first, and take them along with us to the Inventor's place....'

'What for, Gran?' Willard asked her.

'It's time I started doing something useful with my Super-powers. All I've done so far is play around with them, and show off!'

'And what were you going to do, Super Gran?' Edison asked.

'Well, lassie, I'm going to make *all* old folks Super. To give them young, strong, agile arms and legs again. And better hearing and eyesight...all the Super-things I've got.'

This meant one more delay for Edison, but there was nothing else for it, she'd just have to be patient. 'So when do we fetch them?' she sighed, trying to hide her disappointment.

'Right now!' Super Gran told them. 'The sooner the better.'

They jumped off the bus – without upsetting the conductor this time – and took another one, to reach the Old Age Pensioners' club-rooms. But they found that all the Oldies, as Super Gran called them, were away on their annual summer coach trip to the seaside, which Super Gran had forgotten about, in her excitement.

'Oh well,' she grinned, cheerfully, 'we'll just have to fetch them tomorrow. One more day won't matter, will it?'

And so, with the Inventor going to snatch Super Gran...and with Super Gran going to take the Oldies to be made Super – it looked as if tomorrow was going to be a busy day in *all* their lives!

And it was....

8 The Day Begins—Quietly

Edison set off early, next morning, for Super Gran's house, where they'd all agreed to meet. She'd risen earlier than usual to do her morning chores: to prepare her dad's breakfast, do the washing-up, tidy the rooms and make the beds, so that she could be at Super Gran's place as soon as possible.

She'd had a dream, that night, about being chased, along with Super Gran and Willard, by the Inventor and the Super-machine, and she couldn't help thinking that something terrible was going to happen to them. What if Super Gran lost her Super-powers? What if they lasted only a day or two, and then faded? What if they couldn't get the machine back?

She realized her dad was talking to her. 'You're not chasing after that Inventor today again, are you?' he asked, smiling. 'Just be careful, won't you? I mean, you might run into those guys who stole it. That gang.'

Edison's dad was easy-going. He refused to worry about anything – even his best-ever invention being stolen; he left all the worrying to Edison. He didn't really approve of her chasing about after the Inventor, and the machine. She was too young for that kind of thing, he thought, but he always let her go her own way and make her own decisions. As long as she was careful, that was all.

'Don't worry, Dad,' the girl assured him. 'I'll be okay, now I've got Super Gran to protect me. And we'll catch up with that horrid Inventor today, and get your machine back. Super Gran calls him a "scunner", what-ever that is! It's Scotch, I think, but it sounds horrid, doesn't it?'

'I wish you wouldn't waste your time with that machine. *I'm* not bothered about it. I can easily build another one, you know.' He shrugged.

'But I'm *not* wasting my time!' Edison pouted, sternly, hands on hips, determinedly. 'After all the time and money you've spent on inventing it – and then for that rotten "scunner" to pinch it! Oh…oh…!' She was speechless with anger. 'I…I could…could really…punch that man. Really I could!'

Her father laughed. 'Hey, calm yourself, girl. Your face is as red as your hair….'

'It's auburn!' Edison insisted, interrupting.

'I'll build another machine, I *told* you.'

'You're too easy-going, Dad, that's your trouble. And it's not as if the Super-machine's the only invention he's nicked from you. That's about the fourth one! Really, Dad! You're daft!'

The man in the wheelchair shrugged. 'So what? It's only a few little inventions, that's all.' There wasn't much a man in a wheelchair could do about it.

Edison was livid. 'It is *not* all, Dad. You could have made money from those inventions. And *big* money – a fortune – from your Super-machine. I know. I've seen it work, remember. And not just on the budgie, either! I've seen what Super Gran can do with her powers. It's fantastic. It could make you a millionaire! But not if that thieving so-called Inventor gets it on to the market first! Then *he'll* get the fortune!'

Her father laughed. 'It's only money, Edison. It's only money!'

'Yes, Dad, and that's the stuff we need to buy ourselves food and clothes, and to pay the rent and the heating, and everything!'

Really, Edison thought, it was all very well being an inventor with your mind always up in the clouds, like an absent-minded professor, but *some*one had to think of the practical side of things, and that someone was her.

'I'll be off to meet Super Gran, then,' she said, after she'd calmed down a bit.

'Okay, Ta-rah, love. And...the best of luck....' He took her hand, briefly, and patted it, encouragingly.

'Bye, Dad.'

Meanwhile, Super Gran was also setting out early. She was going to go round to any of the Oldies who lived near her, to tell them to be ready to go with her to the Inventor's house, to be made Super. She thought she'd manage that and still be back in time to meet Willard and Edison. So she set out.

Willard, as usual, was snoring at that time of day. He had intended spending the whole day, every day, playing football with his pals, during the summer holidays. But now that he'd found a new playmate, Super Gran, things were different. He'd never have dreamt, before, of going about everywhere with his old granny, although sometimes he'd had to babysit (or rather, 'grannysit') with her, to take her to the shops and to get her pension, and so on. He'd to take her because his mother went out to work, and there was no one else to do it, but he'd leave her, and go off with his pals, as soon as he could. It was cissy, Willard reckoned, to be seen with an old woman hanging on to his arm.

But now that she was a Super Gran, things were different! Willard couldn't be with his gran often enough. He didn't want to miss seeing her play football and chasing crooks and lifting up policemen. She was more fun to be with than most of his pals; and more exciting too!

But he did mind going about all the time with that girl, Edison. He wanted his Super Gran all to himself, he didn't want to share her with a stranger, and a girl at that. And a girl who couldn't play football; couldn't do anything; who tripped over her big feet every time she tried to run, even.

Willard snored on, dreaming of the adventures Super Gran had had already, and the ones she was going to have in the future.

The Inventor was having rather a bad start to his day. Benny 'phoned him to say that *he* would manage along okay, but the Toughies wouldn't be available until later in the day, as they had a spot of thieving to fit in, first thing in the morning!

Still, the Inventor thought, he and Tub and Benny would manage all right without the Toughies. Surely one tough guy, one gentleman (the Inventor), and one timid youth would be enough to tackle and kidnap one little old lady, Super Gran or not! That's what *he* thought!

If this was rather a bad start to the Inventor's day, he was going to find that it would get worse as the day went on!

Tub decided to take a long lie-in that morning. Just to get his own back at the Inventor, for all the running about he'd had, for nothing, the day before. Besides, he had the feeling that the Inventor might try, after all, to get him to help them to kidnap Super Gran...and that just wasn't on!

Twice a week, on Mondays and Fridays, Super Gran and one of her neighbours, Mrs Preston, took their mid-day meal together; on Mondays in Super Gran's house, and on Fridays in Mrs Preston's. But today, which was Friday, Mrs Preston had to go into town, to see someone in the Post Office about her pension. So she thought she'd let Super Gran know that she couldn't lunch with her. She set off to go to Super Gran's house, to tell her.

When Edison reached Super Gran's house she found the front door lying open, slightly. 'That's funny,' she said, out loud. She pushed it further open. 'Super Gra–an!' she sang out. 'Are you i–in?' There was no reply. 'You wouldn't think she'd leave her door open. *Any*one could go in.'

The door swung open far enough for Edison to see

into the hall, where she saw a small hall table lying on its side, on the floor, and a vase of flowers smashed on the carpet.

Edison, hearing footsteps on the path behind her, swung round.

'What's up? Where's Gran?' It was Willard.

'Something must have happenned. Look!' Edison pointed.

They stepped into the hall. Willard picked up the table and Edison lifted the flowers off the carpet, watching out for the broken glass.

'What...what's h–happened?' Willard's voice quaked.

'Looks like there's been a struggle,' Edison replied.

Willard looked into all the rooms – living-room, bedroom, kitchen and bathroom – to see if Super Gran was, in fact, in the house. But she wasn't. 'There's no sign of her,' he said.

Edison thought about her dream. 'It's the Inventor! He's kidnapped her, or something! I had this dream, you see, and....'

'Don't be daft! What would he do that for?'

'I've just got this feeling... ' said Edison, worried.

9 Super Gran Gets Kidnapped?

The Inventor, half-an-hour before this, was calling at Super Gran's house, with tough-guy Benny. Tub, of course, hadn't turned up, but the Inventor reckoned that the two of them, armed with a net, a rope and a large chain, should be enough to capture even a Super little old lady!

He didn't realize he was making a mistake, not having Tub with him. For Tub knew what Super Gran looked like – and he didn't!

They arrived in the Inventor's old, battered, rusty banger of a car at Super Gran's house, knocked on the door and had it opened by a little old lady. She was certainly small in height, the Inventor noticed, but she was plump, quite fat, in fact, which rather surprised him. He'd imagined, from what Tub, Mrs Bottomly and the newspaper girl had said, that Super Gran was a thin, frail old woman. Still, he thought, it doesn't matter, does it?

'Yes?' she snapped, biting the word, like a biscuit. 'What is it?'

'Oh…ah…um…ahem…we're sorry to bother you, madam….'

'Well?' She was more bad-tempered than he'd imagined her to be.

'There's…ah…um…a gorilla….'

'What? A what? Speak up! Don't mumble! A what...?'

'We're from the Chisleton Zoo,' he lied. 'We're from the zoo and we...ah...believe there's an escaped gorilla in your back garden....'

'What? An escaped gorilla?' the little old lady snapped. 'You've no right losing gorillas in other people's gardens! What's the idea?'

'Yes, well....' He was taken aback, somewhat. 'Er...may we come in through your house, to capture it?'

She looked at the net, rope and chain, which fitted in perfectly with the Inventor's 'cover' story. 'No, you can't. It's not....'

The Inventor interrupted her. 'Hurry up or it'll get away!'

'Go round the side of the house!' she told them, annoyed, as the Inventor put one foot in at the door, to stop it being closed on him. 'You'll catch it that way.'

'Oh...ah...well, you see....' The Inventor had to think fast. 'You see, I've sent another keeper round the side of the house. *We* want to come this way, to trap it – see?'

'Oh well,' she mumbled and grumbled. 'Well, all right then. But be quick. I'm going....' She opened the door wide to admit them. 'It's not my....'

Suddenly she found herself pushed back inside the house, the door slammed shut behind them, a rope being wrapped around her and the net being thrown over her.

'Here!' she protested. 'What d'you think you're

doing? What's going on? Stop it! Help! Police!'

The Inventor put his hand over her mouth, to silence her...and she promptly bit it! He howled with pain, pulled it away and tied a hankie over her mouth instead, as a gag.

While the Inventor had been struggling with the little old lady, Benny had been securing the rope around her. The Inventor was pleased, but surprised, to see that they had got this far without too much of a struggle.

'It doesn't look as if we'll need the chain after all,' he said, a bit puzzled. '*I* don't think she's strong at all, do you? She's just like any other little old lady. I don't know what all the fuss was about. I don't know what Tub and Mrs Bottomly kept going on about – I don't think there's anything Super about her.' It certainly puzzled him. Surely *every*one couldn't be wrong?

'Mmm...mmm...mmm...' muttered the little old lady, angrily, from behind her gag, her eyes gleaming with rage.

Then the answer struck him and he snapped his fingers, excitedly. 'I've got it! It's worn off! Her Super-strength's worn off! I never thought of that.' He laughed in triumph. 'We've got her now, all right.' He gloated, rubbing his hands.

'Huh?' muttered Benny, who thought, and spoke, very slowly. 'Wot you...talkin' about...Professor? Wot...strength, like? How d'you...mean, like?'

'Oh...um...never mind, Benny, I'll tell you later.' He hadn't told Benny too much about Super Gran's powers, in case it alarmed him and put him off coming

86

here to kidnap her.

'Come on,' he urged Benny, 'let's get her into the car and back to my place.'

But if they thought they were going to kidnap a little old lady just like that, they were mistaken. For the little old lady wasn't giving in without a struggle. As well as mumbling angrily behind her gag and rolling her eyes at them, she'd also been twisting and wrenching at her ropes, trying to escape from them. And now she began to kick out at her captors, catching the Inventor on the knee and Benny on the shin.

'Ouch! Aaah! Yeek!' they yelped in pain, as they hopped about, nursing their bruises.

And it was then, in the struggle, that the table got kicked over, and the vase of flowers sent flying – the way Edison and Willard discovered it.

'Ugh!' yelled the Inventor, as he was hit in the eye by a little old fist. 'Come on, Benny,' he yelled, 'get… her…out…out…the…door….'

'Crikey!' Benny gasped, struggling with her. 'Wot a…tough little…old lady, like!'

The Inventor and Benny were too busy struggling to get their captive out of the house, down the path and into the car, to notice they'd left the front door open, which was why Edison found it that way, shortly afterwards.

While Benny held the little old lady still, struggling and mumbling, in the back seat, the Inventor jumped into the driver's seat, and drove off. The car zoomed down the street, in a cloud of thick, black, oily smoke, and went into the main road and through the traffic for about a mile. Suddenly it screeched to a halt, as a thought struck the Inventor.

'Hey! What are we bothering for?' he asked no one in particular. 'If the Super-ray's effects have worn off...then she's no longer a Super Gran! So what am I worrying about? What are we kidnapping her for?'

'Wot?' said Benny, stupidly.

The Inventor turned to the little old lady. 'Has the power worn off you?' he asked.

She didn't answer him, and it was a few seconds of mumbling and rolling of eyes and twisting of face before he realized she still wore the gag – and *couldn't* answer. The Inventor was fairly clever at pinching inventions – but otherwise he was thick!

He removed the gag. '*Has* the power worn off?' he asked her, again. '*Aren't* you a Super Gran any more?'

'I don't know what you're talking about, you...you horror!' she snapped. 'Super Gran? What's a Super Gran? What are you talking about? And where are you taking me? And what was that cock-and-bull story about a gorilla? And what do you mean by....'

'*You* should know what a Super Gran is,' the Inventor said, interrupting her. '*You're* the one who's claiming to be one.'

'Nothing of the sort!' she retorted. 'And now, remove this rope and take me home – before I call the police! I don't know what your game is, but it's....'

'*I* know!' The Inventor had had another thought. 'You've lost your memory, that's it. You've lost your memory as well as your strength. That must be what happens. Side-effects. When you lose your powers your

memory goes too.'

He smiled as yet another thought struck him. 'But that's all right. You can't remember being a Super Gran. So you won't be able to tell anyone, will you?' He gloated. 'Let her go, Benny.'

Benny untied the rope and opened the door to let her out. 'Can she...find 'er...way 'ome...Professor, like?' he drawled, slowly. 'I mean...if she's...lost 'er...mem'ry, like? Does she...know where...she lives, like?'

'*Course* I haven't lost my memory,' the little old lady snapped. 'I don't know what you're all talking about. Super Grans! Strength! Memories! You're all mad! Mad! Mad!'

She climbed out of the car and started to walk away. 'Of *course* I know where I live. Where I've lived for the last thirty years – at 19 Highview Road, that's where. Just wait till I tell the police about you lot! Just wait!'

The Inventor didn't wait to hear any more. The little old lady was liable to take a note of his car number. So he zoomed away, before she could think of it.

The car travelled about another mile down the road before the little old lady's last words hit the Inventor, like a slap in the face. 'She said "19"!' he exclaimed.

'Yeah,' Benny agreed, 'nine...teen. That's...where we...snatched 'er...from, like.'

The car screeched to a halt once more, catapulting the unsuspecting Benny forward over the seat in front, to land with his head on the floor and his legs in the air.

'It was Number 23 we were at, not Number 19!' the Inventor yelled. 'So if *she* lives at 19, we picked up the wrong little old lady! She was in the wrong house! *She* wasn't the one we were after! *She* wasn't Super Gran! No wonder she didn't have any strength! That was the wrong woman! No wonder she didn't know what I was talking about....'

Benny muttered to himself, under his breath, as he hauled himself up off the floor, back into his seat: 'Huh! That makes...two of...us, like! I don't...know wot...'e's talkin'...about either...like!'

The Inventor sighed, swung the car out from the kerb to do a U-turn in the road, to return to Highview Road, to pick up the real Super Gran. 'We'll have to go back for the *real* one...' he began, but he wasn't paying enough attention to the traffic, his mind being too busy with two Super Grans, and he swung the car round too far...and struck a passing lorry!

It was only a small crash, but the lorry driver and his mate – who were both bigger than Benny, even! – argued with them and threatened them with a punch-up, for half-an-hour, which delayed their return trip to Highview Road to kidnap the *real* Super Gran....

10 Super Gran Seeks the Inventor

Super Gran had arrived back at her house, to find Edison and Willard looking worried.

'I've been round all my friends, telling them to be at the park this afternoon for a surprise. A "Super" surprise!' she laughed. 'By then we'll have found out where that Inventor scunner lives.'

'Super Gran!' exclaimed Edison, in relief. 'So you're all right after all?'

'Aye, of course, lassie. Why shouldn't I be all right? I've never felt better!' She flexed her muscles.

'We saw the mess, and...' began Willard, but Super Gran went on:

'I couldn't find my friend Mrs Preston, from Number 19. She must be out somewhere, but I'll see her later.'

'Super Gran we thought you'd been...' Edison began.

'Kidnapped!' Willard finished.

'Kidnapped? Me?' Super Gran laughed. 'But why should *I* be kidnapped? Who would want to kidnap *me*? Who would *dare*?' she thundered, flexing her muscles even more.

'That Inventor would,' Edison explained. 'We found your door open and the hall table knocked over.'

'A burglar?' Super Gran suggested, scowling.

'We thought maybe that rotten Inventor had kidnapped you. You see, I had this dream that he chased us...' Edison began.

'Huh! A dream!' Willard snorted.

At that moment the little old lady arrived. She was tired from walking home, her feet were sore and she was furious at being kidnapped. She kept muttering to herself: 'Those cheeky devils! What did they think they were playing at? Gorilla, indeed! No strength! Lost my memory, indeed! I won't forget what *they* look like, I won't! Super Gran...!'

'Oh, Mrs Preston, come away in, dearie.' Super Gran put her arm round the old woman's plump shoulders and led her into the living-room. 'What happened?'

Mrs Preston was raging. 'I've been kidnapped, that's what!'

'Huh! Some "kid"!' Willard muttered.

'What's that?' Mrs Preston was ready to snap the head off anyone who didn't give her all their sympathy, just then. In fact, to be honest, Mrs Preston tended to be like that *all* the time, kidnap, or no kidnap. But she was worse just at that moment.

'Nothin',' Willard murmured, stifling a giggle.

'What happened?' Super Gran repeated, as she ushered her friend into a big, easy chair.

'These two horrible men – gangsters – took me away in a car. Tied me up, they did, and pushed a dirty hankie in my mouth. Ugh!' she shuddered.

'Tut-tut!' Super Gran sympathized. She turned to Edison. 'Will you make us all a nice cup of tea, girlie?' She nodded towards the kitchen, indicating where it was. Then she turned to her friend again. 'Who were the scunners? Do you know them?'

While Mrs Preston told them all about her kidnapping, Edison dashed back and forth between the living-room and the kitchen, making the tea and trying not to miss any of the details.

Mrs Preston explained that when she'd called at Super Gran's and found her out, she'd let herself in with a spare key, to leave a note for her. Before she could get the note written she heard a knock at the door, two men forced their way in, tied her up, gagged her and took her away in their car.

'Och! That was terrible, dear,' Super Gran murmured.

'And they kept on about me being strong, or something,' Mrs Preston scowled. 'And they called me Gran, or Super, or something,' she added indignantly. 'Super-something-or-other. It's just not good enough! Humph!'

'Oh-oh! So it *was* me they were after,' Super Gran said, thoughtfully. ''The Inventor?' she wondered.

'You? Why you?' Mrs Preston snapped. 'What do they want *you* for?'

'Och! I forgot you didn't know, dear. I haven't seen you since Monday, have I? And a lot's happened since then. Well, you see, I'm Super now. I've got Super-strength and Super-speed and....'

Super Gran told Mrs Preston all about the happenings of the previous two days, while Edison served the tea and biscuits.

'I never thought he'd want to kidnap me,' Super

Gran admitted, when she'd finished telling her story. 'I wonder why?'

'Sounds as if he's desperate to meet you, Gran!' Willard grinned. 'Maybe he's heard all about you!'

Super Gran grinned back at him. 'Well, I'm just as desperate to meet him!' She turned to Edison. 'Aye, I think it's about time we all met this famous Inventor of yours that I keep hearing about.'

'Oh yes, Super Gran, let's go!' Edison jumped up, eager to get back on the trail of the Inventor again. 'But he's not *my* Inventor – if you don't mind....' She frowned.

'Right! Come on, then!' Super Gran also jumped up, more quickly than Edison had jumped up. 'Let's get the wee bachle! Are you ready, Mrs Preston, dear?'

'Me? What for? Where am *I* going?' She glowered.

Super Gran pulled her friend out of her chair. 'You want to get revenge on yon kidnappers, don't you? Those scunneryheads?'

Mrs Preston nodded grimly. 'I certainly do....' Her face screwed up.

'Right! Come with us and I'll make you into a Super Gran – like me!' She turned to the children. 'And you two come along and watch the fun!'

'Oh boy!' Willard exclaimed. 'Smashin'!'

'But Super Gran, it mightn't *be* fun,' Edison warned her. 'You'll have to be careful. That rotten old Inventor'll have that gang helping him. Remember – the ones who pinched the machine from Dad?'

'Ach! Don't panic, lassie! You're always panicking, so you are! Just remember who I am! Come on!'

As the others hurried out of the house, Edison shook her head and smiled. 'You're an awful wee woman, Super Gran, so you are!'

Half-an-hour later, after Super Gran and company had left the house to go in search of the Inventor, the Inventor came in search of Super Gran.

'You're too late,' a neighbour at Number 21 told him, after he'd jumped out of the car, run up the path and pounded furiously on the door. 'They left a while ago.'

The Inventor muttered under his breath.

'I don't know what's going on here today, honest I don't,' the woman continued. 'Folks dashing here, and folks dashing there. Coming and going, and going and coming.' She looked more closely at the Inventor. 'Here! Weren't you the one that was here this morning? Eh?' She stopped and waited for the Inventor to offer some explanation for all the dashing about. But he didn't. He just glared at her, made an angry murmuring kind of sound in his throat, turned on his heel and stamped off down the path again.

'Huh! I don't know *what's* going on, I don't,' she continued, speaking to herself. 'All this running about. Boys and girls, and Mrs Preston, and Mrs Smith, and men in cars, and goodness knows who all else....'

The Inventor, ignoring her, jumped into the car and drove off, muttering to Benny: 'This just ain't my...I mean, isn't my day, that's all. This just isn't my day!'

Super Gran and company took a bus to the park, and Super Gran led them to the place where she'd been sitting when the ray hit her, making her Super.

'What are we doing here?' Mrs Preston barked, impatiently.

'This is where it all started,' Edison explained, 'and the ray must've come from one of those big houses over there. The ones that back onto the park.' She pointed to the houses nearby. 'Isn't that right, Super Gran?'

'Aye, that's right, dear,' Super Gran agreed.

'But which one, Gran,' Willard asked. 'Do you know?'

'Shouldn't be too hard to find,' Super Gran told him.

'Couldn't you use your X-ray eyes, Super Gran?' Edison asked.

Super Gran giggled. 'I keep forgetting I've got them. Right then, here goes. Stand back!'

She placed her hands on her temples, which seemed to help, and she 'studied' each of six houses in turn. One of them *surely* was the Inventor's house.

She studied the houses for about ten minutes, during which time Mrs Preston kept nagging her for results.

'Wheeesht!' Super Gran silenced her. 'Let me concentrate.'

Then Willard, getting bored, took a tennis ball from his pocket and began to practise his dribbling. He wanted some action.

Presently, Super Gran said it could be one of *three* houses, and pointed to them.

'Yes, but which one?' grumbled Mrs Preston, impatiently. 'That's not much help, I must say! Humph!'

'Does she always grumble as much as this?' Edison

whispered to Super Gran, who nodded and made a face. 'Can't you "see" the machine, is that it, Super Gran?'

'Aye, I can, lassie. That's the trouble! I can "see" some sort of machine in all three of them, so I can't be sure which one is the Inventor's house.'

'What's the man's name?' Mrs Preston snapped at Edison. 'We could ask a neighbour, or someone. Come on, girl, tell us!'

Edison shrugged. 'I don't know his name. He's always just been known as "the Inventor".'

'Humph!' Mrs Preston snorted. 'A big help you are, I *must* say!'

Edison was beginning to dislike Mrs Preston and was annoyed by her constant moaning. She glowered at the woman.

'Maybe they've *all* got Super-machines in them?' Willard suggested, as he dribbled the ball near them. He was a bit fed up with the whole thing, by now. He was wishing that Super Gran would stop wasting her time on this Edison girl and her Inventor geezer and would play football with him instead.

'Don't be a silly, Willie!' Edison retorted. 'How could they?'

Willie didn't like being called that; especially by Edison. 'Oh, shut up, you. You…you big feet!'

'Shut up yourself, big head! Think you can play football…that's all you *can* do…' Edison retorted.

'That's more than you can do! All *you* can do is trip over your big feet! Red-head! Ginger!'

'It's not ginger – it's auburn!' Edison corrected.

'Here, here, here!' Super Gran yelled at them,

grabbing each of them by the collar and threatening to bang their heads together. 'That's enough of that, Willie…and you, Eddie….'

'Ha, ha! Eddie!' Willard laughed.

'Here!' Super Gran shook him. 'That's enough!'

They calmed down. Neither of them liked being called 'Willie' or 'Eddie', and they knew that if Super Gran banged their heads together, well…it didn't bear thinking about!

They walked from the park to the street where the three most likely houses stood, Super Gran explaining that the machines she had 'seen' might be TV, radio or hi-fi record equipment and that she'd have to get a closer look at the houses, to find out which was the Inventor's house, with the Super-machine. She told them to call at each house with some excuse, keep the housewife 'blethering' and she'd get a better, closer 'look' at each of them.

The first house they tried had stereo record equipment, so that wasn't the one. But, just as they were leaving, Edison spotted Tub walking along the road, past the gate.

'Shhhhh!' She put her finger to her lips. 'It's that fat boy again. The one who was outside the bank.'

'So what?' Willard asked.

'Maybe he's connected with the Inventor?' she suggested.

'Why should he be?' Willard scoffed.

'Aye, maybe he is. He could be. We'll follow him, just in case,' Super Gran said. 'Don't let him see us….'

The woman who lived there wondered what on

earth was going on. First of all she'd opened the door to a red-haired, cheeky-faced girl, a boy dressed as a footballer, bouncing a tennis ball, and a cross, grumpy, little old lady. They'd asked her if she'd like to join an old folks' club! Cheek! And her only forty-nine, too!

Then they'd gone down the drive, to be joined by *another* old woman, thinner than the first one, and smaller; barely taller than the children, with a tartan tammy on her head at a jaunty angle...where had *she* come from? From the back of the house, perhaps? Now, what was *she* up to? What were they *all* up to?

They reached the gate, drew back, went into a whispering huddle and then tiptoed silently after a fat boy who'd just passed by in the road, outside.

Was *she* mad, she wondered – or were *they*? She wasn't sure whether to call the police, or an ambulance, for them!

11 Super Gran Meets Tub Again

Tub arrived at the Inventor's house. He put his hand through the letter-box and pulled out the key, which hung on a string, and opened the door. He stepped inside, closed the door and decided to raid the larder while the Inventor and Mrs Bottomly were both out.

Then the doorbell rang.

He turned back, opened the door and saw Super Gran with those two kids standing there – plus another little old lady! Where did they find all the little old ladies, he wondered?

'There he is!' Edison exclaimed, pointing. 'The fat boy!'

'It's not fat, it's muscles!' Tub scowled, automatically. Then he slammed the door shut in their faces, in panic.

That there Super Gran was haunting him, he thought. Was following him everywhere! Was after him! Or was it the Inventor she was after?

So Tub did the only thing he could think of, on the spur of the moment, when he slammed the door shut. As if a mere closed door could stop a determined Super Gran! Tub should have known better!

Just as at the bank, Super Gran didn't stop to think...with almost the same result! She merely pushed forward on the door, forgetting she had Super-strength, and it crashed forward, flew off its hinges and toppled over on top of Tub, who had thought he was safe behind a closed door.

Super Gran didn't stop. She plunged forward over the top of the fallen door – and the fallen Tub! – and then stopped, inside the hall, puzzled. Tub had disappeared!

Then she realized. She turned, picked up the flattened door and pulled the flattened Tub out from under it!

As she yanked him to his feet, Tub groaned. 'Ooh! What happened? What hit me?' He staggered about, dizzily, clutching his ample stomach, which now had ample pains in it!

'Oh, I'm sorry, laddie,' Super Gran apologized, as she 'dusted' him down. 'I keep forgetting about my Super-strength! I didn't mean to run you down. Are you all right?'

'All…right…?' Tub gasped, breathless. 'I feel…as if …I've been…run over…by a…train!'

The trembling Tub was wondering again, briefly, about his self-defence. But what use was it against this human dynamo? It would take a real expert to use judo or kung-fu or anything else against Super Gran. For a start, she never stood still long enough!

'Wow!' Willard exclaimed, impressed.

'Another door ruined!' Edison giggled.

As Super Gran turned to answer them she took her eyes off Tub, and Tub summoned up the strength to attempt an escape. He limped hurriedly away from the group, through the long hallway and turned the corner at the end, disappearing from sight.

'*Now* where is he off to?' Super Gran sighed as she dashed after him. 'Och! I wish he'd stop running away every time he sees me. I only want to *talk* to him....'

She zoomed round the corner after him and caught up with him. '...Just talk to him – about his boss, the Inventor!'

'So he *is* connected with the Inventor!' Edison said, when the rest of them in turn had caught up with Tub and Super Gran again. 'And this *is* the Inventor's house? But how did you know?'

Tub stopped outside a door marked 'Workshop' and had turned to face Super Gran, his arms held up against the door and his legs spread wide apart, as if blocking her way into the room.

'Who else but an Inventor would have a "Workshop"?' Super Gran grinned. 'Besides...I read his mind!'

'What?' Willard exclaimed. 'When?'

'That's another Super-power you've got, Super Gran!' Edison enthused.

'He thought about the Inventor just before he shut the door in our faces,' Super Gran explained.

'I...what?' Tub started. Then he thought he'd be loyal to his boss, in the hope of getting his back-pay. 'You...you can't come in here. It's private.'

'So this is where the machine is hidden, is it?' Super Gran smiled. 'Good. That's one question I won't have to ask you, laddie!'

'Is the machine in there, Gran?' Willard asked.

'Well, Willie, he's not guarding the cat, is he?' She

guffawed, loudly. 'What's your name?' she asked Tub.

'I…I…I'm…I'm not telling you!'

'Och, let's see now….It's Algernon Everton McGuire, isn't it?' she grinned.

'H–how…how did you know that?' Tub was shaken. 'I–I didn't tell you….'

'I *can* read minds! I was just trying it out!' Super Gran clapped her hands, like a little child, pleased with herself. 'I sort of "heard" him saying: "I'm not telling that old bat I've got a daft name like Algernon Everton McGuire. Even Tub's better than that!" '

Tub clapped his hand to his mouth, as if he *had* said that, and didn't want to reveal any more.

Mrs Preston, who had been silent for a while, and hadn't even been grumbling, glowered at everyone, and now pushed through between Willard and Edison to grab Super Gran's arm. 'Look! Why don't you get on with it! Whatever it was we came here to do! I'm tired of all this nattering. Are you going to do something, or aren't you?'

'Aye, dearie, you're quite right,' Super Gran agreed, while Willard muttered, under his breath:

'Silly old moaner!'

'What was that?' Mrs Preston, who wasn't fond of Willard – or any other child, for that matter – glared at him.

'Right then, Tub, laddie,' Super Gran said, turning back to the youth again. 'Don't let's waste any more time…or doors! Open up and let us in. You *know* how easy it is for me, if you refuse!'

Tub shrugged and gave in. What was the use? He'd

105

only get flattened again. 'What d'you want it for, anyway?' he asked, as he opened the door and they all trooped into the cluttered room.

'I only want to make old folks young again, and strong. Like me,' she beamed. 'I'll start with my friends, then I'll do all the oldies in town, then in the country – then the world, who knows?'

Tub wondered when the Inventor would get back. He was supposed to be out kidnapping Super Gran, but here she was – in his own house – talking about using the Inventor's own machine. If Tub could keep Super Gran talking until his boss got back, then *he* could deal with her, and stop her using it, somehow. It was the Inventor's problem, after all, not his.

But Super Gran, of course, read Tub's mind as soon as he thought his thoughts. And she smiled, quietly, to herself. It was more like *her* dealing with *him*! But she said nothing. She'd just humour Tub, and string him along.

'Yes,' Super Gran continued, 'my plan is to help *all* the oldies. Even *your* grannies…you have a wee granny or two, have you?'

'Will you hurry up and get on with it?' Mrs Preston nagged, impatiently. 'Never mind all this chat!'

Willard, like Mrs Preston, was getting bored again with all the talk, and was looking for more action. He went to examine the Super-machine, which was more or less just a large box, with wires and coils sticking out, all over it; and a gun-like nozzle or barrel sticking out at the front; and a control panel with switches, buttons and levers, at the back.

'It's not very fancy, is it?' He was disappointed. 'Huh! It doesn't look as if *that* could do anythin'!' He had been expecting something like the elaborate gadgets they had in all the best science fiction serials on the telly. 'That's just a load of old rubbish!'

'What!' Edison was indignant at the very idea of Willard daring to criticize her father's greatest invention. She secretly admitted that the machine *was* a bit amateurish-looking; but it *did* work, after all. And she wasn't going to admit to him that it could be more glamorous-looking. 'It is *not* a load of old rubbish! It works, doesn't it? Look at Super Gran.'

She was going to say something else, and Willard was getting ready to give her a cheeky answer, but they both caught sight of Super Gran taking a step towards them, threateningly, as if to bang their heads together, so neither said another word. They just scowled at each other.

'Tell me, lassie. How does it work, do you know?'

Edison shrugged. 'Not really. It's got something to do with that button there,' she pointed, 'and that switch.'

'Och! We'll soon find out!' Super Gran said, cheerily. 'We'd better get on with it before Tub's scunnery friend the Inventor gets back.' She went over to the machine.

'You're not scared of *him*, are you, Gran?' Willard asked, unable to believe that she'd be scared of anyone.

'I am not!' Super Gran was indignant at the very idea. 'But the Inventor's out with some of his gang, looking for me. And he's going to turn his gang into

Supermen – to help him to rule the world, if you please! So we'd better get a move on.'

Tub clapped his hand to his mouth again, realizing that he must have thought all those things about the Inventor and his gang.

Super Gran pointed to the far wall. 'You stand over there, Mrs Preston, dear. I'm going to make you into a Super Gran.'

'About time, too!' grumble-mumbled her friend, as she shuffled over to the wall, opposite the machine.

'I'll press this button...I think. And pull this switch...I hope...and, hey presto!' She giggled. 'Or, rather – hey Preston! You'll be a Super Gran!'

Mrs Preston, now that her time had come, at last, had lost her impatience and was nervous. 'Are...are you s–s–sure it'll w–work all r–right? I mean, will it hurt me?' She trembled.

'Of course not! It just tickles a wee bit, that's all,' Super Gran assured her, with a giggle. 'But do keep still, dearie, or the ray'll miss you!'

'Will you make *me* Super, Gran?' Willard asked, beaming.

Super Gran frowned. 'Mmm, well now, I don't know about that. It works on adults all right, but we don't know what effect it'll have on youngsters, do we?'

'Aw, go on, Gran,' Willard coaxed, as the machine glowed and hummed and warmed up. 'Just a *little* bit Super, eh? Just a *wee* bit?'

But Super Gran shook her head. 'No, no, laddie, we'd better leave it until we've checked with the lassie's dad. He'd know best, wouldn't he, lassie?'

Edison nodded, and this just annoyed Willard all the more.

'Look, Willie, you can do me a wee favour and save us some time. Go with the lassie and fetch the old folks here. I told them, this morning, to meet me at the park gates, just down the road. Bring them back here and we'll make them all Super! Okay?'

'Aw, Gran, couldn't *she* go? We don't *both* need to go.' He wanted to stay and watch Mrs Preston becoming Super, but Super Gran told him he'd see the other Oldies being made Super, once he'd fetched them back.

She ushered them out of the door. 'And hurry!' she said, hoping they wouldn't fight all the way there, and back. They just didn't seem to hit it off together, she thought. She shrugged. It couldn't be helped.

So the youngsters went to fetch the Oldies, Willard muttering under his breath all the way.

Super Gran went back into the workshop, found the machine ready – and operated it. The blue ray shot out, turned Mrs Preston blue for a few seconds, and then died away.

She led the old lady to the room's only chair. 'Just sit down for a wee while, dear, till the tingling and tickling stops. It won't take long. Okay? Cumfie?'

Then, after staring through the back wall of the room, with her X-ray eyes, towards the garden, she turned to Tub.

'Come on, my laddie,' she said, taking his arm and walking him towards the door. 'Come with me.'

Tub, while things had been happening, had been silently munching his usual diet of chocolate bar. Now

he was slightly taken aback. 'Who – me? Ah... um...where to?'

'Into the garden. There's something I want to show you.'

She led him out of the house – over the flattened door, which made Tub wince at the memory of being under it – and round to the jungle which the Inventor called the back garden.

'What is it?' Tub asked.

'Patience, laddie, patience!'

She led him to the garden hut which she had 'seen' through the wall of the workshop. She pushed him inside, slammed the door shut, locked it, and then looked for a large piece of wood to jam it shut, just in case.

'Hey!' Tub complained. 'What's the idea?'

'That'll keep you out of the way, for a wee while, while I get on with making people Super!' she told him, as she walked away.

While Super Gran was out in the garden with Tub, things were happening indoors!

12 Super Gran Meets the Inventor

After the Inventor and Benny left Super Gran's house, the second time, the Inventor accidentally ran his car into a hole at the side of the road. Which, on top of the earlier mishaps, rather angered him, to say the least! Then, the half-hour wait for the break-down truck didn't help his temper.

'Pity we…didn't have…your friend…with us …like,' Benny had drawled, slowly.

'What friend?'

'Old lady…wot's-'er-name? That there…Super Gran, like!'

The Inventor's face turned scarlet at the mere mention of her name. He ranted, and raged, and thundered at Benny.

And then, when they finally arrived back at the house and the Inventor saw his flattened, battered front door, he ranted and raged and thundered all over again!

'It ain't…your day…Professor, like!' Benny sympathized.

They'd arrived at the house exactly at the time when Super Gran was leading Tub 'up the garden path', so they didn't see her and didn't know she was there.

'What the….' The Inventor was speechless on seeing his door.

'Looks like...a tornado's...struck, like....'

'Oh no!' The truth dawned on the Inventor. 'It was....'

'It was...a tornado...like?'

'Not exactly! It was that woman...that confounded Super Gran woman! Who else could've done that? *She* must've been here! Must've got her powers back! But when did she do it? And how did she know where I lived?' He was thoroughly puzzled. 'Come on....' He led the way to the workshop. 'The machine....'

He threw the workshop door open – and saw their little old lady, Mrs Preston, of course – sitting quietly on her chair. Benny hung back. He had seen what Super Gran had done to the door, hadn't he?

'So you *are* Super Gran, after all?' the Inventor said, in triumph. 'And you *were* just acting daft this morning? Lost your memory, had you? Hadn't any strength left, hadn't you? Didn't know what I was talking about, didn't you?'

When he looked round and saw that the Super-machine was switched on and was humming away, he knew why she was there; or he thought he did! Her Super-powers *had* run out, he thought, and she was there to get a 're-fill'. Then, he thought, she really *had* been powerless that morning and had somehow found her way here, to get at the machine again.

But hang on, he thought, if she was powerless ...how had she managed to smash the door down? He shrugged. No matter.

He switched the machine off and stepped towards her.

'Mind out...Professor,' Benny warned him, slowly. 'If she's...Super Gran...you'd better...mind out ...like....'

Mrs Preston said nothing; she just silently fumed!

'Oh, don't worry, Benny!' The Inventor was confident now. He took another step or two nearer her. 'She's here because her strength has run out and she wants to renew it. Only we got back in time to stop her! She hasn't used the machine yet!'

And that, of course, was where the Inventor was wrong! For, of course, she *had* used it. And it was just then that Mrs Preston decided to go into action!

She recognized her kidnappers when they'd entered the room and she was boiling mad at them. She'd let the Inventor rave on, but now she thought she'd show him how wrong he was about her!

She stood up, not quite knowing what she was going to do – but don't worry, she'd think of something! She'd had this funny, tingling feeling in her bones, and all through her, and the odd feeling that she could do *any*thing now, just like Super Gran. So she'd try...and see what happened!

And what happened was: as the Inventor reached her, a superior smirk on his face, Mrs Preston's hand shot out, grasped his arm...and threw him over her shoulder!

She was almost as surprised as *he* was! And the smirk froze on his face!

'Ugh!' he groaned, then: 'Help!' It was all he had time to cry before she grabbed him again.

She picked him off the floor, by the arm, and swung

him round in an arc, before letting him go. And this time he landed on top of Benny, and they both crashed against the wall, and slid slowly and gracefully to the floor, side by side!

'Ouch!' Benny moaned, and: 'Oh…oh…oh!' the Inventor moaned.

'Humph! That'll teach you to hit little old ladies,' the little old lady snorted, as she picked up the chair she'd been sitting on, and threw it at them.

Benny and the Inventor ducked and tried to defend themselves as the chair smacked into the wall above their heads, and shattered into dozens of pieces, showering down on them.

'No! Stop! Help! Police!' the Inventor cried.

Mrs Preston, getting carried away with her new-found strength, turned to grab hold of one of the smaller work-benches, full of tools, vices, motors, and bits and pieces of equipment – to throw *that* at the men. But neither of them waited to be hit by it! They scrambled to their feet, colliding against each other as they did so.

'Bully *me*, would you!' Mrs Preston yelled as the men dived towards the door, together, getting jammed between the door-posts. 'Kidnap *me*, would you!'

They looked back over their shoulders, terror on their faces, and saw her with the bench in her arms, ready to throw it. They squeezed through the doorway and escaped into the corridor, just before the bench shattered against the wall above the door.

'And next time don't pick poor, defenceless, little old ladies!' Mrs Preston muttered. Then she giggled a bit at what she'd said. 'Humph! *I'm* not a poor, defence-less, little old lady. Not now. I'm a Super Gran now!'

She jumped nimbly over the ruined remains of the work-bench and leapt out into the corridor, to chase the men. But they had already dashed along the corridor, round the corner, through the hall and were, at that moment, running towards the flattened front door...where they met the *real* Super Gran, returning from the garden!

At long last Super Gran and the Inventor came face-to-face with each other. But the Inventor didn't recog-nize her, not having seen her before. As far as he was concerned, this was just one more little old lady. A smaller, frailer, more fragile-looking one. But he soon found out differently!

'No! Not another little old lady!' the Inventor yelped. 'The house is polluted with them! Come on, you – mind out the way!'

'Oh, hello...' Super Gran started to say, all friendly and polite. For she, in turn, didn't know who the Inventor was either, for that matter. But she didn't get the chance to finish her greeting.

The men had had enough, and were stopping for no one. So they pushed her aside, to get past; to escape from Mrs Preston. But they didn't know who they were trying to push around!

The Inventor pushed Super Gran one way, while Benny tried to push the other way, knocking her off-balance. But not for long! The old lady recovered, and spun round.

Then she put a hand on each of their backs and she

pushed, hard! The men flew through the air, through the open doorway, over the flattened door – and landed in the bushes outside, head-first, their feet sticking out, kicking madly in the air!

Super Gran rubbed her hands together, just as Mrs Preston dashed round the corner, into view.

'There!' Super Gran said. 'I don't know who those scunners are – but that'll teach them some manners! That'll teach them to go round pushing poor, innocent, harmless, little old ladies about!'

Like Mrs Preston, Super Gran giggled at the thought that those words – 'innocent' and 'harmless' – hardly described *her*!

'*I'll* tell you who they are,' her friend snapped. 'They're the devils who tried to kidnap me, that's who they are!'

'What?' Super Gran swung round to her friend.

'Yes. And *I* wanted to be the one to pulverize them,' Mrs Preston grumbled. 'What have you done with them?' She sounded peeved.

'Nothing much! I just gave them a wee push, that's all.'

Super Gran dashed through the open doorway, to tackle the men again, now that she knew who they were but, for once, she was too late. The Inventor and Benny, desperate to escape, had climbed out of the bushes and zoomed down the path, fear almost giving them Super-speed, towards the front gate and the safety of the Inventor's battered old car.

'Come on!' Super Gran yelled. 'The Inventor! That must've been the Inventor!' She ran out of the house, closely followed by Mrs Preston.

They reached the street, chased after the car, and were within a few yards of touching it when Edison, Willard and ten Oldies appeared from the park, blocking their way.

'Watch out! Out of the way!' Super Gran shouted, as she and Mrs Preston almost collided with the group.

By the time the two Super Grans disentangled themselves from the crowd of Oldies, the Inventor's car was too far away for them to catch it.

'Och! Never mind!' Super Gran grinned. 'I'll get the rotten wee scunners the next time.'

She turned to lead the Oldies into the Inventor's house. 'Besides,' she grinned hugely, 'it'll give me a chance to make you all Super – while he's out of the way. Come on, let's be having you....'

13 The Super-Oldies

When Super Gran told the Oldies she was going to
make them Super, like her, they were all a bit scared.
But once she and Mrs Preston explained what it was
like being Super, and had shown them some of their
Super-powers, the Oldies changed their minds and
couldn't wait to be made Super. When they realized
they'd regain their failing eyesight and hearing and
would get new Super-strength in their tired old muscles, they were *really* keen to give it a try.

So Super Gran put them in front of the machine, one
by one, shot the blue ray at them – and ended up with
another seven Super Grans and three Super Gramps!

Afterwards, Super Gran discovered *she* had Super-
powers which the others didn't have; her X-ray eyesight and her mind-reading ability, for instance.

'Maybe that wee bachle of an Inventor altered the
machine after I was made Super,' she suggested.
Which, of course, he had done, while fiddling with it to
check that it would make Super Gran normal.

'Couldn't you look inside the machine and see if
anything's been altered?' Edison said.

Super Gran did this, with her X-ray eyes, but,
naturally, she couldn't detect any changes. But it did,
however, give her an idea. She opened the machine,
removed a small lever and then checked that it

wouldn't work without it.

'Good!' she exclaimed. 'The Inventor won't be able to work the machine now, unless *I* let him do it. And I won't. I'll be taking it back to the lassie's dad.' She explained to the Oldies that it was really *his* machine.

By now the Oldies – or, rather, the Super-Oldies – were eager to try out their new strength, and were lifting benches and heavy tools and things. But they didn't have enough room to do it there, especially since Mrs Preston had rather wrecked the workshop!

'Go into the garden,' Edison suggested. 'There's plenty room there.'

'Good idea!' someone said, and everyone trooped out to the back garden, where some of them started lifting each other; and others lifted heavier objects, like filled dustbins, concrete slabs and a garden roller!

'Jings, folks!' Super Gran exclaimed. 'You're doing fine.'

'Gran,' Willard tugged her sleeve, excitedly, 'why don't we have a competition? For *all* the Oldies? You know, football and runnin' and jumpin' and weight-liftin' and things like that?' Action was more in Willard's line, rather than standing about, chatting.

'Good idea, Willie boy,' Super Gran enthused, 'but there's not much room in the garden for that.' She looked round the 'jungle'. 'And the grass is too long, and everything.'

'We could go over into the park,' said Willard, pointing towards the wall at the foot of the garden. 'It's over there.'

'Yes, let's do that,' the Super-Oldies agreed, excitedly.

'Aw, Super Gran,' Edison frowned, 'what about the machine? I thought we were going to take it back to Dad?'

'We can have a wee bit of fun first,' Super Gran told her. 'And besides, the scunner can't use it if I've got this wee bit....' She showed Edison the lever, then replaced it in the pocket of her suit.

'We could have our own Super-Oldies Olympic Games,' Willard suggested. He was cheering up, now there was a chance of a bit of running about and, who knows, maybe even a game of football?

The Oldies began walking along the side of the Inventor's house, to reach the street, to go round to the park gate. But Mrs Preston stopped them in their tracks.

'Where are you going?' she snapped, as always. '*I'm* going *this* way – it's quicker!' She pointed towards the garden wall.

She ran towards it – it was about six feet high – and leapt right over it! 'Wheeeee!' she yelled excitedly, like a child, and for once, not grumbling about anything. 'This is the life!'

The other Super-Oldies followed her example, one after the other, jumping the wall as if it were only six *inches* high!

'Hey!' Willard yelled, indignantly. 'What about *me? I'm* not Super! *I* can't jump like that!'

'I'll jump you over – both of you,' Super Gran volunteered, including Edison in her invitation.

'Oh no, Super Gran,' the girl protested, concerned,

as usual. 'Not both of us at once. You'll strain yourself.'

'Blethers! I can do *any*thing – haven't I told you?'

'Yes. Often!' murmured Edison, smiling.

'Jings!' Super Gran exclaimed, suddenly. 'I'd forgotten all about poor old Tub!' She went over to the hut, removed the wood, unlocked the door, and Tub staggered out.

He had dozed off in the hut. He was tired out, after all the running about and excitement he'd had with Super Gran. He had woken up only a few minutes previously, in time to see the Super-Oldies doing their various 'things' in the garden, watching them in amazement.

'Crikey! There's dozens of 'em!' he muttered, blinking, unable to believe his eyes. 'Where'd *they* all come from?'

Meanwhile, Super Gran had lifted Edison and Willard, together, one under each arm, and had jumped them over the wall. But there was no one else in the garden as they jumped. So no one noticed the small object which fell out of Super Gran's pocket, as she jumped – no one, that is except Tub!

He hurried over and picked up the lever which Super Gran had removed from the machine, although he didn't know what it was. 'Better hang onto this,' he murmured. 'It might be something important.'

The Inventor decided not to return to his house until he and Benny had collected the Toughies. The next time he came face-to-face with Super Gran and her friend he, like the Scouts, would 'Be Prepared'! It would be five against two which, to the Inventor, was a fairer fight!

The Inventor had to keep reminding himself not to call the Toughies 'Rough', 'Tough' and 'Gruff' to their faces. Otherwise *they* might do something to *his* face – like, for instance, punch it!

He smiled, gleefully, as he thought about the Toughies. Rough and Gruff were over six feet tall, and, although Tough was only five-feet-two, he was as broad as a bus! And they always walked around with the tall ones one on each side of the small one in the centre, as if protecting him. And these rough, tough, mean baddies had broken noses, scars and flattened ears, having been in dozens, hundreds probably, of fights in their time.

Yes, he thought, in delight, the Toughies were just the boys to put those two Super Grans in their place. Especially – and he smiled an extra-gloating smile at the thought – especially after he'd made them into Super-Toughies. No one, but no one, would be able to stop them then!

As the Inventor's car stopped outside his house the Inventor leaned across the front-seat to whisper to Benny: 'Get the Toughies...er, I mean...get your boys to go into the house ahead of us, Benny.'

'Eh? Wot...for, like?' Benny blinked at him, stupidly.

The Inventor didn't want the three Toughies, who were squashed together uncomfortably, knees together, shoulders hunched up, in the back seat, to hear him. 'Well, I mean...there might be someone

...ah...um...waiting for us, in there....' He nodded towards the house, and winked. But it took some time before the slow-thinking Benny understood what he was on about.

'The Super Grans!' the Inventor hissed. 'The Super Grans! And we know what *they* can do, don't we?'

At last, Benny's face broke into a smile of understanding. 'Oh, yeah, I...see, like. Sure, Professor...sure, like....'

The Inventor and Benny hung back, timidly, as the Toughies went on ahead, up the path towards the house.

'Wot 'appened 'ere?' Rough asked, in a rough sandpaper voice, as they stopped and goggled at the flattened front door.

'Ah...would you believe...two little old ladies?' the Inventor asked, slowly.

'Ugh?' exclaimed Gruff, gruffly – which was all that Gruff *ever* exclaimed! And the other Toughies roared with laughter.

'No, I didn't think you would!' the Inventor went on. 'But watch out for them, just the same...!'

The five of them made their way to the workshop, the Toughies still leading the way – just in case – with Tough guffawing, at the top of his voice: 'LI''LE OL' LADIES? EH? LI''LE OL' LADIES? WOT NEXT, EH? WOT NEXT?'

The other two joined in the laughter, but the Inventor and Benny knew better...and had the bruises to prove it!

14 The Super-Toughies

The Inventor sighed with relief when they reached the workshop. Not only were there no Super Grans about, but also the precious Super-machine was still there, and was all in one piece. Luckily the little old Super Gran who had attacked them hadn't gone completely mad, and smashed the machine to bits.

He switched it on and told the Touchies to pick up the work-bench and all the gear which Mrs Preston had thrown around.

'Let's see if the machine's all right,' he said.

'WOT 'APPENED 'ERE?' Tough bellowed. Tough *always* bawled, when he talked, having worked in a noisy factory where you had to bawl to be heard.

'Was it the li''le ol' ladies again?' Rough rasped, in his coarse, hoarse voice, laughing. And the others joined in.

The Inventor pressed a couple of buttons. 'Once it warms up we'll get started.'

'STARTED?' repeated Tough, deafeningly.

'Started?' Rough echoed, raspingly. 'Started on wot?'

'Ugh?' said Gruff, gruffly, as usual.

'Started on making you all into *Super*-Toughies…er, that is…*Super*men,' the Inventor explained.

'Wot d'you...mean, Professor...Supermen...like?'
Benny asked.

The machine should have been working by now.
What was wrong with it, the Inventor wondered.

'How would you like to be tough, rough and...?' He
stopped himself in time, just before he'd said, '...and
gruff'. 'Ah...um...that *is*, how would you like to be
tough – I mean...*really* tough?'

The Toughies looked at each other. They frowned,
puzzled – and then annoyed. They glared at the Inventor.

'BUT WE *ARE* TOUGH!' roared Tough, thumping
one huge fist into his other palm with a huge, deafening thud which made the Inventor jump with fright.

'Yeah! We *are* tough,' rasped Rough, agreeing. He
picked a metal bar off a bench and bent it, without
batting an eyelid. 'Who says we ain't? Huh? Who says
we ain't?'

'Ugh?' Gruff muttered, as always, bringing his ugly,
scarred, battered face threateningly within an inch of
the Inventor's. The other two also closed in on him.

The Inventor edged back, nervously. 'What...what I
m–meant w–was – *Super*-tough. How would you
like to be *Super*-Tough?'

He wished the machine would warm up and rescue
him from the angry Toughies, who thought he was
insulting them.

'Oh, you're back then, boss?' It was Tub, from the
open doorway, munching a huge 'triple' cheese sandwich.

'Tub? Where've *you* been all day?' his boss demanded. 'Always the same. Never around when you're wanted!' He didn't really want Tub. He just shouted at him, to show the Toughies that he too was tough, in his own little way.

'Me?' gulped Tub, indignantly, swallowing a mouthful of sandwich in surprise, and choking on it. 'Me? Where have I been all day? I'll tell you where I've been all day. I've been....'

'Not now, Tub, I'm busy.' The Inventor ignored him *and* the Toughies, turning his attention to the machine again.

'I was flattened under the front door...!'

'Not now!' repeated his boss, staring, puzzled at the machine. It definitely *wasn't* warming up properly.

'And she read my mind, and....'

'Not *now*!' The Inventor raised his voice as he became more and more puzzled. And more and more vicious – he kicked the machine.

'And I was locked up in the hut for hours on end....'

'NOT NOW!' The Inventor was shouting now, as he examined the machine which simply refused to work, even after the kick.

'And I found this on the grass. She dropped it, and....'

'NOT NOW, TUB!' The Inventor roared at the top of his voice, without even glancing at Tub *or* the lever he held in his hand. 'I'M BUSY! GET LOST!'

Tub shrugged, shoved the lever into his pocket and shuffled off, munching his sandwich. 'Huh! That's all the thanks you get for trying to help. Might as well get meself something to eat...I'm starving!'

The Inventor, watched in silence by Benny and the scowling, palm-thumping Toughies, continued to fiddle with the machine, giving it another kick and a couple of slaps. He took the front plate off, getting into the works, where he probed and searched amongst the wires, looking for a loose connection. Eventually, he found what was wrong.

'Hey! There's a piece missing! A lever! Won't work without it! Where on earth did it go to?' He scratched his head, puzzled. 'Come on, don't just stand there, looking ugly,' he ordered Benny and the Toughies. 'Help me look for it. Must've dropped somewhere.'

He couldn't understand how it *could* have fallen out, but he couldn't spare the time to wonder about it.

So Benny and his boys, mumbling and grumbling, got down on their hands and knees and searched all over the place; under the tables and benches; *on* the tables and benches; under the Super-machine; all over the room.

Finally, the Inventor decided to look for a bit of metal which he could readily shape into a lever, which would do instead of the missing piece. He rummaged through the drawers, through boxes full of bits and pieces, and through cupboards. But he was out of luck. He didn't have another bit of metal which was roughly the size.

While this search was going on, Tub re-entered the room, munching a 'triple' banana sandwich, this time!

His boss looked up. 'Ah, Tub – have you seen a piece of metal about this size – and this shape…?' He held up two fingers in a 'C' shape, to show Tub the size and shape of the piece he wanted. 'I need it for the machine. There's a piece missing.'

'Oh, you mean…' mumbled Tub, between mouthfuls of sandwich, '…like this?' He drew the lever he'd found out of his pocket.

His boss's face brightened. 'Ah, that looks just about right.' He took the lever and placed it in the slot where it fitted perfectly – naturally!

Suddenly – it dawned on the Inventor. 'You great fat, hairy dumb-head, Tub….'

'Not fat…muscles!' muttered Tub, showering them with crumbs.

'That *is* the lever!' The Inventor ranted and raged. 'Where did *you* get it? What were *you* doing with it? What did you remove it for? What's the big idea? What d'you think you're playing at?'

He went on at some length, while the machine, at last, began to warm up. Tub, swallowing a mouthful of sandwich, waited patiently until the man stopped for a breath, and then he said: 'I found it. In the garden. On the grass. Super Gran dropped it. When she jumped the wall. Into the park. I found it.'

'Why didn't you tell me?'

'I tried to….'

'Rubbish!'

'I did. I told you. You wouldn't listen. You never do….'

Tub shrugged, sighed. What was the use? He sat on a bench, munched the rest of his sandwich and watched while the Inventor turned Benny and the Toughies into Super-Toughies. And then, after the Inventor had

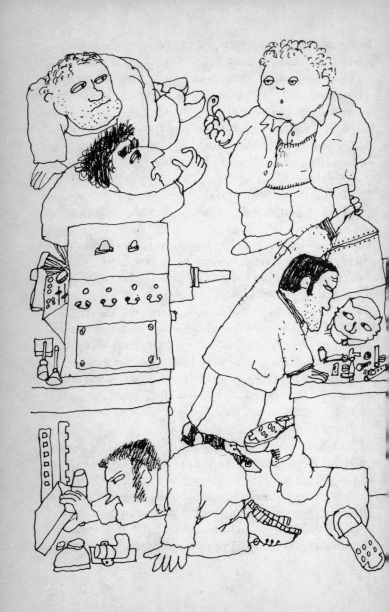

made himself Super, he told Tub he was no longer needed. He was sacked! Fired! Dismissed!

'But...but what about my six-months' back-pay?' Tub asked.

'You've had it!' the Super-Inventor snapped. 'I never intended paying you anyway. See!'

Tub left the house, and, a few minutes later, the Inventor and the Toughies also left, heading for the park...to capture the Super Grans.

When they reached the park gates the Inventor stopped and listened and, with his Super-hearing, he heard the sounds of the Super-Oldies having their Super-Olympic Games. 'That sounds like them over there. Come on! This way!'

Tub, trailing along behind them, dejectedly, to see what happened, muttered to himself: 'Look out, Super Grans. You haven't a chance against this bunch!'

But then, suddenly, he brightened. He remembered that there were only five on the Inventor's side – and there were a dozen on Super Gran's side. And even *Tub* could see that the Inventor was outnumbered. And the Inventor didn't know it – yet! Tub grinned at the thought of what would happen.

Tub was now completely on Super Gran's side. To be sacked, and given no wages, and after all the bumps and bruises he had received at the hands of Super Gran, too; being rugby-tackled, flattened by doors, shut up in huts, having his mind read – and called fat! He was furious with the Inventor, and longed to get his revenge on him, somehow.

Meanwhile, the Inventor and his gang of Super-

Toughies had sneaked into the park and were dodging through between the trees of a small wood, to spy on the Super Grans, before jumping out to capture them.

But when the Inventor saw there weren't *two* Super Grans, but *twelve* of them, he just about fainted! 'What the...?' He counted them, twice, to make sure he wasn't imagining them. 'Twelve of them...? How on earth...?' He was speechless.

'Thought there...was only...two of...'em, like?' Benny whispered in his slow drawl.

'So did I!' the Inventor snapped, in reply.

'Wot do...we do...now, Professor...like?' Benny asked. Even *he* could see that they were outnumbered twelve to five.

The Inventor thought it over. 'Well, *we* can't capture them all and fetch them back to the machine. So we'll have to fetch the machine out here, to them.'

'FETCH THE MACHINE...? Tough yelled, but was 'shushed' by the Inventor.

'Out here?' rasped Rough.

'Ugh?' said Gruff.

The Inventor turned to the Toughies. 'Benny and I will stay here, to keep our eyes on the Super Grans. You three go back for the machine – you'll manage it easily. And cover it with a sheet, so they won't see what it is.'

'OKAY' bawled Tough.

'Professor,' added Rough.

'Ugh!' agreed Gruff.

They set off to go back for the machine, to make the Super-Oldies normal little old ladies and gents again.

15 The Super Battle Commences

The Super-Oldies had been holding their Super-Olympics in a quiet part of the park, a large stretch of grass almost completely surrounded by trees, in the shape of a horseshoe. They'd chosen this area because it was quiet and there was nobody about; they didn't want a crowd of ordinary, non-Super, people standing around staring at them.

While the Super-Oldies had been racing their races and jumping their jumps, Super Gran and Edison had gone shopping to a little general store near the park gates; they'd bought cakes, pies and lemonade, for a picnic.

After a while the Oldies, tiring of races and jumping, had a tug-o'-war, with a rope they 'borrowed' from a park-keeper's hut. Then they borrowed a large, heavy grass-roller which they used for weight-lifting contests. And when they tired of that, they had a tree-climbing competition.

And it was when the Inventor saw the Super-Oldies doing these things, from where he was hidden amongst the trees, that he realized just what the five Super-Baddies were up against.

Presently, Edison persuaded the Oldies to sit on the grass and have their picnic which, she thought, would give them a bit of a rest, after all their exercise and excitement.

'Isn't it great,' one little old Super-lady said, as she hungrily munched a pie, 'to be as fit and strong as this at our age!'

'Not 'alf!' a little old Super-gent replied. 'I'm fit enough to climb Mount Everest!'

'And I'm fit enough to *run* up it!' joked a second man.

'Then why don't you?' asked a little old lady, smiling.

'I would,' he grinned, 'but I don't know which bus takes you there!' And they all laughed.

'Huh!' exclaimed yet another little old Super-lady. 'Who needs a bus? I could run all the way there!'

'With the bus on your back!' quipped one of the men.

Super Gran, sitting with the others on the grass, glanced over to where three men, in the distance, were carrying a large square box, covered with a big white sheet, which had a bit sticking out at the front. She frowned. She thought it looked somewhat familiar. 'I wonder...?' she murmured, quietly. She trained her X-ray eyes on the box for a few seconds, then: 'Jings!' She leapt to her feet. 'It's the Super-machine!'

'What?' Edison looked up. 'What is it, Super Gran?'

'Those wee baehles over there – in the distance,' she pointed towards them. 'They've got the Super-machine!'

'Oh no! They're stealing it! Dad won't get it back!' The girl jumped to her feet, and the Oldies did the same, one by one.

'How can three men carry it? Isn't it too heavy?' a little old Super-lady asked.

'Maybe they're Supermen!' Willard laughed.

'Maybe they are!' Super Gran agreed, grimly; *she* wasn't laughing. 'I'm going to listen to them, with my Super-hearing.'

She tuned in, and heard:

'When's that there Inventor twit goin' to let us try out some of these there Super-power wotsits we're supposed to 'ave?' Rough grumbled, in his grating-gritty voice.

'YEAH,' Tough yelled in agreement. 'ALL WE'VE DONE SO FAR'S LUG THIS GREAT ROTTEN MACHINE ABOUT. AN' FOR WOT?'

'Ugh!' mumbled Gruff, also in agreement.

'S'pose we'd better 'elp 'im first, to get rid of those there troublesome old folks,' Rough said.

'YEAH,' little Tough agreed. 'SUPPOSE SO.'

'Ugh!' murmured Gruff, also in agreement.

They continued to carry the machine towards the trees, where the Inventor and Benny were hiding.

When Super Gran heard this conversation she paled. 'Oh no!'

'What's wrong, Super Gran?' Edison asked, frowning.

Super Gran saw Tough pointing towards the part of the wood where the Inventor was lurking. She looked in that direction, with her X-ray eyes, and after a few seconds she spied Tub creeping along between the trees; and then, a bit further on, she spotted the Inventor and Benny, looking out towards the Oldies.

She studied them intently for a few seconds, and then she said, urgently: 'Come on, everyone – we've got to get out of here – fast! Quick! Run!'

'But…but what *is* it?' Willard asked.

'Yes,' Mrs Preston snapped. 'What is it *now*? There's always something!'

'Come on – hurry!' Super Gran urged them along.

The Super-Oldies, panicking, were blundering around, bumping into each other, puzzled and worried by Super Gran's behaviour, and by the sudden turn of events. 'What's wrong?'

Edison went to run, tripped and fell – as usual! 'Oof!' she grunted. 'But…but what's the matter, Super Gran?'

'It's the Inventor! The scunnerylugs!' she yelled, pointing in the Inventor's direction. 'He's in among those trees! That's his gang! With the machine! They're going to make us normal again! I've just read his mind! Come on…run…!'

Super Gran, the Super-Oldies, Willard and Edison rushed across the clearing towards the trees at the far side, a few hundred yards away – away from the Toughies and the Super-machine. But the 'youngies' couldn't keep up with the Oldies! Edison kept falling! And even Willard couldn't keep pace with them. So Super Gran stopped, came back, swooped them up, one under each arm, and then chased after the Super-Oldies again.

'But Super Gran,' Edison pointed out, 'you took that part out of the machine! So it won't work! So why are we running?'

Super Gran stopped once more, dumped the children on the ground and searched through her suit pockets. 'Jings! You're right, lassie. I'd forgotten that! I've got a Super-memory, and I don't think! Now, where did I put it…?'

But, of course, her pockets were empty. The lever wasn't there. 'I *thought* I'd put it in there,' she sighed.

'You did, Gran, you did,' Willard assured her.

'You must've lost it,' Edison told her, 'with all that running and jumping about, it must've jumped out of your pocket.'

Super Gran broke into a grin. 'Never mind. As long as *he* hasn't found it, then *he* can't use it! So we're all right!'

'Yes, Super Gran,' Edison said, 'but what if he *has* found it? Or has another part like it?'

'I'll soon find out,' Super Gran replied, turning to face the machine and looking at it with her X-ray eyes.

As she did so, the Inventor and Benny dived out of the woods, towards the machine.

'Oh-oh! They *have* got it – or a part like it, anyway! Bump-jumpit!' she cried, picking the children up again and starting to run after the others. 'Jings! Here we go again!' she exclaimed, grimly. 'Never a dull moment!'

As soon as the Inventor reached the machine he switched it on, and danced about impatiently, waiting for it to warm up. 'Hurry up, hurry up!' he yelled at it. 'Stupid machine!' He kicked it.

'Will it…work out…here, Professor?' Benny drawled. 'There ain't…no elect…ricity, like….'

'Don't worry. It'll work off its batteries for a while. When it finally warms up, that is! Confound it!'

140

He gave the machine another kick to encourage it to get going. 'Run as fast as you like!' he shouted at the escaping Oldies. 'You'll never outrun the Super-ray!'

At last, the machine, having grumbled and groaned, came to life. Its lights flickered and flashed, and it hummed noisily.

'Ah! That's me beauty!' the Inventor crooned, as he turned the barrel towards the Oldies, took aim...and fired!

'Spread out!' Super Gran shouted to the others. 'Don't all bunch together! He can't hit us all if we spread out!'

The Oldies obeyed, and spread out, but, thinking they were outside the range of the Super-ray, they stopped running. Which was a mistake.

'No, no, don't stop!' Super Gran yelled at them. 'Keep running!' But she was too late!

The machine's yellow normalizing ray shot out, hitting the Oldies, one after the other, as the Inventor directed it towards each of them, in turn, in an arc, as if firing a machine-gun.

'Run! Run!' Super Gran urged the Oldies, but when they tried to run again they found they were ordinary, normal, little old men and women again, unable to walk fast, never mind run!

'Come on!' the Inventor yelled at Benny and the Super-Toughies, 'Get Super Gran!' And the gang charged after her.

Super Gran; off to one side of the other Oldies and not yet hit by the Super-ray, dropped the children, told them to run to the safety of the woods and picked up the Oldies' tug-o'-war rope.

She turned and charged at the Super-Toughies, whirling the rope round and round above her head, like a lasso. She whirled it so fast – at Super-speed – it acted as if it had hardened into a heavy, solid piece of metal rod. And the Toughies, not realizing what they were facing, charged forward, right into it!

'Come on, you wee bachles! Come and get it!' Super Gran cried.

The Super-Toughies were no match for the Super-whirling rope, and down they went, all four of them, in a heap.

Super Gran, yelling: 'Cha...a...arge!' leapt over the fallen Toughies and charged towards the Inventor at the machine.

16 The Super Battle Continues

The Inventor was horrified to see his gang, the whole of his Super-army – being felled by a little old lady with a piece of old rope! He was furious! 'Huh! I can't trust *any*one to do *any*thing properly! I've got to do everything myself!'

And this was his mistake. For, instead of merely aiming the Super-ray at Super Gran and making her normal, he wanted to show off! He wanted everyone to see what a big, strong, brave, speedy Super-Inventor he was! So he left the machine, to charge towards Super Gran, to grapple with her. After all, he thought, *he* might as well try out *his* Super-powers...everyone else had!

And this, in turn, gave Tub his big chance!

Tub had followed the Inventor and Benny through the wood, had hidden behind a leafy bush and had seen everything that had happened, so far. He'd wondered what he could do to help Super Gran and the Oldies, now that he was firmly·on *their* side. But he'd decided to wait, meantime, until he could think of something.

He had, of course, thought about rushing out at the Inventor, with his famous, but so-far-unsuccessful, karate. But he'd thought better of it. After all, if it didn't work against his seven-year-old sister, it wasn't likely to work against a Super-Inventor, was it? Even

143

Tub realized that.

But now, as the Inventor left the machine unattended, Tub saw his chance.

He leapt out from behind his bush, dived towards the machine, and he pulled the switch from the 'normal' position back to the 'Super' position. Then he aimed the barrel once more at the poor, confused Oldies, starting with Mrs Preston, who'd been moaning and grumbling to anyone who'd listen, about losing her Super-powers.

The Inventor had dived towards Super Gran, but the old lady had side-stepped, tripped him up and sent him crashing, face-first, onto the grass. Then she'd jumped on him, winding him, and looked round for someone else to tackle.

Mrs Preston felt herself tingling with Super-powers again, as did the others, and she too looked round for someone to tackle.

Super Gran saw the Toughies had recovered from her 'rope trick', were scrambling to their feet – looking for trouble – and decided to go for them again. 'Cha…a…arge!' she yelled, to her Oldies. 'Get the wee scunnerylugs!'

The Oldies didn't really know who the Inventor was. They didn't know he wanted to rule the world. All they knew was that, for some reason or another, this Inventor man was trying to rob them of their Super-powers – and they were having none of that! They were going to *keep* their Super-powers! So they charged to attack him, and his gang of Super-Baddies.

The Inventor sat up, groaned, rubbed his bruised

nose and his winded stomach and looked over to see Tub standing beside the machine. So *he'd* been the one who'd made the Oldies Super again?

'Tub! You great, fat, hairy twit! What're *you* doing there? Look what you've done! Get away from there! I fired you!'

'I know!' Tub grinned an ear-to-ear grin and aimed the ray at the Inventor. 'Now I'm going to "fire" you!' He laughed.

But Tub forgot about the Super-Inventor's Super-speed. The man rolled to one side to dodge the ray, then scrambled to his feet, dived forward, ducked low, reached Tub and lashed out to slap him with his hand. The Super-slap caught Tub, knocked him off his feet, and sent him crashing, backwards, into the wood.

Super Gran, helping the Oldies fight the Toughies, should have been keeping her eyes on the Inventor and Tub; for the Oldies were managing well enough against Benny and his boys.

One of the Super Gramps was whirling the rope, as Super Gran had done, at Benny. Another man was swinging from a tree-branch – like a little old Tarzan – and was hitting Tough each time he swung forward, towards him, with his feet. Two of the Super Grans were attempting to run down Rough with the heavy grass-roller. And poor old Gruff was being clobbered by about eight little old Super Grans with their little old handbags!

So Super Gran, seeing that her Oldies were doing all right, turned back to the Inventor, in time to see him taking over the machine again, from Tub, and aiming it at her....

Meanwhile, Willard and Edison had run to the cover of the woods and had crept round behind the trees, Edison tripping over every tree-root she came across. They arrived behind the Super-machine just as Tub was knocked sprawling into the bushes, by the Inventor.

'It's my dream!' Edison exclaimed. 'I *knew* something terrible would happen!'

'Huh! Dreams!' Willard snorted.

'Ooooh!' Tub groaned. 'What hit me?'

Willard and Edison helped him, with a struggle, to his feet.

'Wow! He's some weight!' gasped Willard.

'He's so fat!' Edison explained.

'Not fat...muscles!' Tub managed to gasp, automatically, between breaths. 'Grr! That Inventor!' he muttered, determined to do something about him, *and* his gang. In a rage, he tried out his karate chop on a small tree branch, then fell about, clutching his injured hand! 'Ow – ow – ow!' he yelped, in agony.

'Don't take your spite out on a poor little tree!' Edison said.

'Don't be daft, that's karate,' Willard told her, as Tub continued to nurse his hand.

'Well, it's not going to help Super Gran much, is it?' she retorted, pointing to where the Inventor, at the machine, was taking aim, once more, to make the Oldies normal.

'And this time,' the Inventor was muttering, 'I'll make them normal for good! Starting with that confounded Super Gran....'

Super Gran Super-ducked down, just as the Super-ray shot out, and it missed her, but hit everyone else – Mrs Preston, the Oldies, Benny and the Toughies! And everyone, all mixed up together at the time, fighting, was made normal again.

As they stopped fighting, swinging from trees, whirling ropes, rolling rollers and clobbering with handbags at Super-speed and became their old, normal, ordinary selves again, they could only stand there and stare at each other, utterly confused.

'Don't panic, lads,' the Inventor told the Toughies. 'I'll make you all Super again...as soon as I've made Super Gran normal!'

And Super Gran, kneeling on the ground, was trapped! She couldn't possibly jump up to run, or dodge away fast enough to escape the speed of the ray, or the Super-speed of the Inventor aiming it at her.

'This one's for *you*, Super Gran! Just for you! You won't be a Super Gran much longer!' He gloated, and took his hands off the machine's controls, to rub them together, in triumph. 'Are you ready? Ready to be a normal little old lady again? Ready to see me start on the road to be world ruler?' He laughed, as he teased her, keeping her in suspense. 'Then, dear lady, here it comes....'

Suddenly, just as he put his hands back on the controls, there was a blood-curdling yell from behind him. 'Aieeeeeeeee!' He looked round, startled.

It was Tub. He dived out from the trees, with Willard and Edison right behind him. All three threw themselves at the man, Tub connecting with a long-awaited, and successful-this-time, karate chop, which hit the Inventor's shoulder and spun him round, away from the machine. Willard dived at his legs and Edison, of course, tripped over Willard but somehow landed on top of the Inventor, winding him yet again.

Super Gran took the chance of this interruption to dive forward, take charge of the machine and turn the Inventor into a *normal* 'scunner' again! And then, quick as a Super-flash, before the Toughies could stop her, she changed the machine to 'Super' again and 'shot' the Oldies, making them Super once more. And then, as a bonus, she made Tub Super, now he'd proved he was on her side instead of the Inventor's.

And so, at long last, Tub became Super.

'Eee, it's all go, isn't it?' gasped one of the Super-Oldies.

'Wish they'd make up their minds, one way or the other!' snapped Mrs Preston, complaining, as usual.

Tub, who was to have been the *first* Super-person, became the *last* Super-person. For, just then, because of being over-used and being continually switched back and forth between 'Super' and 'normal' – the machine finally protested! It groaned, moaned, fluttered, spluttered...and exploded in a shower of blue, red and green flames and clouds of smoke.

'Huh!' Willard complained. 'I won't get made Super now!'

While the Oldies stood around, helplessly watching the machine burning, Edison with tears glinting in her eyes, the Inventor and the Toughies took the chance to

148

sneak off into the woods.

But Tub saw them. And Tub pounced! With a second blood-curdling yell, he flew after them, his karate-chopping hands flailing the air, threateningly. The non-Super-Inventor and Toughies, looking back over their shoulders and seeing the new Super-Tub coming after them, fled in terror!

By now Edison was crying uncontrollably. 'It's all been for nothing,' she sobbed. 'Dad's machine's gone. Ruined! Wrecked! He'll have to start all over again. And he got nothing out of it....'

'Jings, lassie!' Super Gran consoled her. 'What are you going on about? There's always *my* money. Your Dad can use that to help him invent another machine. Okay?' She patted Edison's shoulder, to comfort her.

'Your money? Wh–what money, Super Gran?' Edison sniffed.

'The reward! From the bank! The bank raid! Remember? For me catching those scunner-some bank-robbers?'

Tub strutted back to the group of Oldies, chest puffed out proudly. The Toughies were now in the far distance and the Inventor, who couldn't keep up with the others, was limping along behind them, out of breath. Tub took his self-defence book from his pocket.

'I won't be needing *this*!' He grinned and threw it over his shoulder...and it flew at Super-speed and Super-length...and bopped the Inventor on the nut, sending him sprawling! Tub flexed his muscles, proudly.

'Wow! Some muscles!' cried a little old Super-lady.

'Not muscles – it's fat,' Tub replied, automatically. 'Er…ah…that is….' He'd got it wrong! 'It's not fat, it's…aw, you were right the first time!' He grinned happily.

Someone suggested they'd had enough excitement for one day and it was time to go home, so they strolled through the park, towards the exit.

Willard, still keen for a game of football with Super Gran and the others, asked her: 'What'll we do now, Gran?' hoping she'd suggest more fun and games.

But even Super Gran was a bit tired after all their adventures and had had enough for one day. Tomorrow she meant to start doing something useful for all the old folks – those who hadn't been made Super. Tomorrow she'd stop playing around, she thought.

'Well, laddie, we've got a lot to do. We've got the town's old folks to help, for a start! And we can't make them Super until the lassie's dad builds another Super-machine. But we'll help them some other way.'

'Aw, Gran, no more football and games and things?' Willard was disappointed in Super Gran. He'd expected life to be one huge game, with her around. She'd let him down.

'Och! Why not?' Super Gran relented, grinning. 'Football, cricket, jumping, running, swimming, the Olympics…why not?'

Edison laughed. 'That wouldn't be fair, Super Gran. You and the Oldies would win every game….'

'And a gold medal in every event!' Willard added.

'Och, I'm sure we can spare a wee bit of time for fun and games, eh folks?' She turned to Tub and the Oldies.

'Do you fancy taking on world-class football teams and boxers, eh?'

'Sure thing! Not half! When do we start?' they exclaimed.

The Super-Oldies, always ready for a bit of fun, now they had the health and strength to enjoy it, couldn't wait to get started.

In fact, they thought it was a good idea...a great idea...a Super idea!

But then...that's *another* story!

About the Author

Forrest Wilson was born in Renfrew, Scotland. He began his writing career on scriptwriting for children's comics, progressing to short stories for women's magazines and the radio. After twenty years in various clerical situations, he became a full time freelance writer, concentrating mainly on compiling crossword puzzles for the national, local and trade press. He now lives in Ayr with his wife and teenage daughter.

Some other Puffins

BAGTHORPES UNLIMITED
Helen Cresswell

'I wish to see my children, and my children's children, gathered together so that I can feel my life has not been in vain. I want a Family Reunion.'

This announcement by Grandma Bagthorpe produced a long silence while everyone digested the horrors of what lay in store. There was only one course open to them – to drive the Dogcollar Brigade from the house at the earliest opportunity! More monumental mix-ups and mishaps which follow the other books in the Bagthorpe Saga – *Ordinary Jack* and *Absolute Zero*.

THE FOX BUSTERS
Dick King-Smith

The chickens of Foxearth Farm were a very special lot – they had long legs, they were quick witted, but most important of all, they could fly! They really could fly – up and away out of the reach of foxes.

The Foxearth Fowls found their names on the bits of writing scattered about the farm, like Fisons and Leyland, Trespassers and Beware Of. And one day Massey-Harris became the father of three chicks so exceptional that they were given brand-new names, for Ransome, Sims and Jefferies could fly faster, higher and further than any before them. And when a group of determined young foxes kept laying plans for one fiendishly cunning raid after another, the legendary three found a way of outwitting the most crafty of them. Not for nothing would they one day be known as the Fox Busters!

THE EIGHTEENTH EMERGENCY

Betsy Byars

Benjie and his friend Ezzie have often discussed what they
would do if an octopus or a crocodile attacked them –
but whatever is Benjie to do in the worst emergency of
all, when Hammerman the biggest boy in the school, is
asking for a fight?

Anyone who has ever felt scared at school (and most of
us have at some time) will enjoy this very funny yet
sympathetic history of poor Benjie's terrors, and feel a
relief almost equal to his own when he finally overcomes
them.

DANNY THE CHAMPION OF THE WORLD

Roald Dahl

Danny's playroom was the workshop of his father's filling
station, his first toys were the greasy cogs and springs and
pistons that filled it. By the time he was seven he could
take a small engine to pieces and put it together again –
pistons and crankshaft and all. So being eight was a lot of
fun.

As it turned out, the year he was nine was even more
exciting, for Danny's father had a deep, dark secret, a
secret he had kept hidden all Danny's life up till then,
and soon after he'd revealed it Danny found himself
engaged on a wild and difficult scheme.

A wildly funny, wickedly inventive romp of a book,
suitable for every age.

THE ALMOST ALL-WHITE RABBITY CAT

Meindert DeJong

But now Barney was sitting in a tiny flat in a huge block all alone while his parents were out at work. No rabbits, no Grandpa, no noise at all. Then, at that dullest of all dull moments, he heard a scratchy noise, and a white paw came poking under the hall door, and then somehow or other the lock clicked and opened. It was miraculous! Of all the people she might have visited, this clever, beautiful, talented cat had chosen Barney, the very person who needed her so much.

McBROOM'S WONDERFUL ONE-ACRE FARM and HERE COMES McBROOM!

Sid Fleischman

Josh McBroom would rather 'sit on a porcupine than tell a fib', and when you read the tall tales in this book, that's a good thing to remember, for there are a lot of folk who just don't believe the stories he tells!

For instance, there's the time he bought a farm for just ten dollars – a marvellous bargain, until he discovered that the eighty acres were piled on top of each other like a pack of cards, and were under water too. But then came the hottest day on record, when the sun came out and dried up the water, leaving the McBrooms with one acre of topsoil so rich it ought to be kept in the bank!

Sid Fleischman's collection of stories has a wonderfully funny, earthy folktale quality, and Quentin Blake's illustrations add his own touch of genius.

Heard about the Puffin Club?

... it's a way of finding out more about Puffin books and authors, of winning prizes (in competitions), sharing jokes, a secret code, and perhaps seeing your name in print! When you join you get a copy of our magazine, *Puffin Post*, sent to you four times a year, a badge and a membership book.

For details of subscription and an application form, send a stamped addressed envelope to:

The Puffin Club Dept A
Penguin Books Limited
Bath Road
Harmondsworth
Middlesex UB7 ODA

and if you live in Australia, please write to:

The Australian Puffin Club
Penguin Books Australia Limited
P.O. Box 257
Ringwood
Victoria 3134